True Beginnings

Books by Willow Madison

True Nature

True Choices

True Control 4.1

True Control 4.2

we were one once 1

we were one once 2

Existential Angst

the SAYER

True Beginnings

Willow Madison

Madison, Willow

True Beginnings (True Series, Book Two)

Front Cover Design by David Colon (www.colonfilm.com); Back Cover Design by XIX (www.thenineteen.net)

This is a work of fiction. Names, characters, places and incidents are either the product of the author's imagination or are used fictitiously, and any resemblance to actual persons, living or dead, business establishments, events or locales is entirely coincidental.

This book is intended for adults only. Spanking and other sexual activities represented in this book are fantasies only, intended for adults. Nothing in the book should be interpreted as advocating any non-consensual spanking activity or the spanking of minors.

www.willowmadisonbooks.com

ISBN-13: 978-0-9963191-2-6
ISBN-10: 0-9963191-2-3

1 Him

We're different. Wednesday night, yesterday, it changed everything between us. *It clarified everything.*

I smile thinking of how Lucy was yesterday. *A shaky start, but a good beginning for us.* She was so hesitant, trying to still hold back. She wasn't ready to embrace her new life with me, not completely, not yet. *She was almost there, though.* I'm getting her the rest of the way there.

Yesterday, she was able to give in to what she really wants, submit to her true feelings. We had a nice day together, playing hooky, staying in my bed, ordering food in, and keeping the world out.

I knew seeing her face in a mirror would bring back a little of her fear and maybe some of her anger. She had to get used to seeing herself as mine. That I could do as I like to her, punish her how I want, and she'd accept it. Yesterday, she started to do this...*with my help.*

But today is the true start. Today the world is let back in; rather, Lucy has to face her world from her newly defined role with me. *Today is an important first step for us.*

I hear her bare feet on the tile in her kitchen, but I keep my eyes closed. "Are you going to stay in bed all day, again, ya bum?"

I only open one eye. Lucy is standing with her hands on her hips. She has a bra and thong on, her short robe open in the front, her blonde hair falling in wet ringlets past her shoulders. She also already has on a lot of makeup. It's why I had agreed to sleeping here last night, instead of at my place, so she could cover the red mark on her cheek and bruise under her jaw for work today.

I smile at her and still with only one eye open put my arm out for her to come to me.

She shakes her head and crosses her arms in front. "Oh, no...I'm not getting back in bed with you. We have to go to work today."

I stop smiling and harden my look. She instantly moves to crawl in bed, snuggling in with her back to me. *Things are definitely different between us.* "Good girl." I kiss her head and feel her relax a little more. "Let me see you."

She knows what I mean. Slowly, she rolls over to face me, putting her hands on my chest. I push her hair away from the left side of her face. Taking hold of her chin, I gently turn her face more. Both marks are well covered. The redness on her cheek is already fading, spreading into a lighter shade; the bruise along her jaw isn't as hidden, the blue of the center showing a little, the surrounding yellow covered only a little better. *But her thick hair will cover this.*

I actually *like* seeing the small bruises on her. I worry that this makes me a monster. *I hope my own past won't work its way into our future.* But I know that my love for Lucy is stronger than any violence or anger I've been through.

"You're beautiful." I kiss her nose. She finally raises her eyes to me.

"You...you can't see anything, Max?" She's shaky still. In the dark before falling asleep, she had said she was afraid of her friends seeing something at work, that she wouldn't know what to say to them. I told her not to worry about it. We could stay home together one more day and then she'd have the whole weekend in between the next time she needed to see anyone from work if she wanted. It was her choice.

"No. You did a good job, baby." I kiss her and she melts into me more, relieved. "Just keep your hair down if you don't want anyone to ask you any questions." She stiffens again.

"So you *can* see something?" A hint of defiance has creeped back in her eyes. She drops this quickly though. Her eyes show only fear when she asks, "Aren't *you* afraid of someone asking me about my face?" The shakiness increased in her voice to end in more of a whine.

"No."

She searches my face, my eyes. I don't say more just calmly look back at her. Lucy finally closes her mouth and swallows hard, before blurting out, "Why not?"

I speak slowly. *This is important for her to understand and I need to be clear with her about this part from the very beginning.* Despite my own fears about my anger and my past, this is important for us going forward. "Because if anyone asks you, you'll have to say what happened. Won't you?" The bewildered look on her face again, mouth opening, then closing. I wait until she only nods, slowly. *Good.*

"And what happened...is you misbehaved. Didn't you?" I pause again, waiting longer for her to slowly nod a tiny bit. Her eyes show a hint of the shame that made them so beautifully full of tears Wednesday night. "And I had to punish you. Didn't I?" The pause this time stretches longer. Her hands grow warm on my chest, her cheeks flaring red. She lowers her eyes before imperceptibly nodding.

"Answer me, Lucy." Her head jerks up quickly. *Good girl.*

Her responsiveness to the nuances of my voice and facial changes is still a marvel to me. I only added the slightest amount of sharpness and she is quick to reply, "Yes, Sir...." *She's learning.*

"Lucy, I'll make a lot of promises to you. And I will *always* keep my promises." She nods, relaxing. "I *will* discipline you. And my punishments *will* hurt." I wait for her to relax again. "I will even leave marks on you sometimes to help you remember to be my good girl long after a punishment." I rub her hair; her eyes can't meet mine. "But I will never *harm* you." She looks up questioning now. "I won't damage you. Do you understand?"

She is searching my eyes again. "I think so…"

"I want you to know that you're safe with me. To not question that part."

"I know that, Max."

"Good." I give her a small kiss on her cheek. "I *want* you to be afraid of making me angry…this will help you to remember how to behave." She only nods, a little look of fear and guilt added to her searching eyes. "But I don't want you to be afraid of me truly hurting you. I will never do anything to you…that can't heal without damage." I falter on how to make this clearer without scaring her more. *I want to reassure her, not frighten her this morning.*

She takes her time answering, swallowing several times, "I knew from what you said before…about your family, your beliefs…that you might…that you *would*…do *something* if you were angry with me." She swallows more. Her chin lifts a bit and her eyes focus on mine, "But I know that you love me, Max. And I know that I love you. And I know that I trust you."

I kiss her again and she is even more eager to kiss me back. "You better get ready for work...unless you want to stay with me today again?" I tenderly pull her hair forward, over her shoulder.

"No. No, I'll be okay." I let her get out of bed and watch her select a short-sleeved dress out of her closet. She turns to face me with the dress in front of her, "Do you like this one?" The blue of her eyes pop even more against the pale blue of the dress. She looks anxious to please me. It's one of the ones we bought together.

I give her a big smile, "It's perfect." We're meeting a few of my friends for dinner tonight right after work. I don't know if she remembers this with all that has happened over the last two days. "Remember, we're going to dinner tonight...?"

Her eyes answer before she does, "Oh! ...I forgot..." The look of apprehension is back. She just takes her dress and heads towards the kitchen and attached bathroom. At the end of the bed, though, she turns back to me, "You don't *really* want me to say any of that, do you...I mean...you want me to make something up...if anyone asks...?"

"No, Lucy, I expect you to say exactly what I said." She starts to laugh, but stops herself. Again, she's very quick to respond to the subtle changes in my look. "You earned those marks, little girl. For misbehaving. And I won't have you lying about how you got them." She only lowers her head and turns to walk away again, a puzzled look still on her face.

I don't really want anyone questioning our relationship. *Not this soon, anyway. Not as we're still figuring this out together.* Lucy is just starting to accept so much and there's so much more I need her to accept. But I need her to be clear on this point too. She has to be able to face up to how things are between us now, no matter who questions us.

I know that this part may be the hardest for her. That today may be one of the hardest in our relationship. She needs to understand that I'm not ashamed of what I did, what I needed to do, to her. I punished her for cursing. She knew my rule about her using foul language and I caught her cursing with her friends Wednesday night. So I slapped her, three times. I actually held back anger; since this was the first time I used our new understanding to punish her.

However, she's still fragile, uncertain about how this will work, our new relationship. She still needs a little time to get used to her role, her place with me. *Time and training.*

I smile. *I'm willing to give her both.* I get out of bed and grab my boxers from a chair. I head towards her bathroom. She learned yesterday that I expect her not to close any doors to me. She doesn't have the right to privacy anymore. Her bathroom door is open. *Good girl.*

She has the dress on now. She only half smiles at me as she continues to fluff her curls dry, her part dramatic to cover her left side more. I stand behind her, dwarfing her frame with mine. I zip up her dress and kiss her shoulder, "I like this on you."

"Thank you." Her smile brightens. "Do you need the shower?"

"No. I'm going home and for a run before heading to work." I move to stand in front of her toilet; she blushes and starts to leave the bathroom. "No. Stay. Keep getting ready." She hesitates for only a second before going back to looking at herself in the mirror, avoiding looking my way. I have to think of something besides her cute shyness to be able to pee.

2 Her

Leaving my apartment, Max locks my door, but doesn't put the key into my outstretched hand. "I'm going to make copies of both our apartment keys today."

"Oh...Okay..." *I've never had a key to a guy's place before*. All my boyfriends have either had roommate rules against it or didn't want that much commitment. I've also never given a key to a guy before. I correct myself...*I'm not giving it; Max is taking it.* Another way that he is taking control. I don't say anything more, just head slowly down my steps to the street.

I stop in front of my gate and wait for Max to open it. I know this is one of his pet-peeves, that a gentleman opens doors. And again, I'm shocked by how much things have changed in such a short amount of time. How much I've changed.

The last two days have been intense. I never could have imagined him slapping me, let alone me accepting it as punishment for breaking one of his rules. *But he did...and I did.* And now I'm forever changed somehow. *I think and feel differently.* It's all about Max, pleasing him, not disappointing him...not angering him.

I can feel the happiness bubbling in me when he kisses my cheek as he opens the gate. I'm proud of myself for remembering this simple thing that makes him so happy. Proud of myself for not disappointing him by reaching for the gate myself.

I'm surprised to see Jeff waiting at my curb. "How did he know to be here?"

"I texted him last night. He's been waiting only a little while." Max heads to the left side of the car and Jeff opens the door on my side for me. I smile as he greets me. I've definitely gotten used to having a private driver. Using cabs and buses when I'm not with Max feels strange now.

Inside, the smell of coffee and pastries is overwhelming. I didn't realize how hungry I was until now; I was so distracted with everything that Max said this morning. I lean forward and say, "Thank you, Jeff. This coffee is just what I needed." He only smiles in return. I turn to Max and give him a kiss on the cheek, "Thank you for thinking of this." I know it's really his doing. His attentiveness to me, his caring nature, is what I fell in love with first.

"You're welcome, baby." I laugh as he tickles my knee with a squeeze.

In front of my office building, Max stops me from getting out of the car. Jeff waits patiently a step away with the door open. "I'll pick you up at 6:30. Sharp." His look of warning sends that familiar shiver of excitement down from my stomach. *Another of his pet-peeves...being on time.*

I only nod in response, but his look further darkens, so I quickly add, "Yes, Sir." And I'm rewarded with one of his big smiles. He kisses me one last time.

My boss walks by just as I get out of the car. She stops for me to catch up. "A private car? I must be paying you too much." She's laughing, the Tigerlady with her fangs out.

"Oh...No...It's my boyfriend's." I hurry to keep up with her longer legs. She's always in a rush and expects everyone to be at her pace in everything.

"Hmmm...How nice," and her laugh is cut off by the revolving door. I roll my eyes while she can't see me.

I've been dreading lunch all day. I know Tracy and Laura will stop by my office to see which spot we're going to today. We always try to have lunch together, but especially on Fridays. Tracy calls it the pre-party to our weekends.

I thought about skipping out early, but I knew this would be more suspicious and lead to even more scrutiny and questions from them. Besides, since Max and I have been dating, I've seen less of them. Laura already told me how upset they both are by this.

I jump when I hear a loud knock on my open door, "You ready for lunch? Geez, someone's had too much coffee today." I turn and Tracy is standing with her knuckles still against the doorframe, Laura right behind her.

I grab my purse from a drawer and head out; but not before Kevin, my officemate, adds behind me, "She's been jumpy like that all day, girl." He laughs and shakes his head, not taking his eyes from his computer screen though. I only roll my eyes in response, ducking my head down more, as I pass Tracy out the door.

Laura puts her arm in mine. "I like your hair today."

I mumble a small, "Thanks," keeping my head down, since she's on my left.

I've made it through most of lunch without either of them commenting on anything. *I think I'm in the clear.* I don't really know what I'd say if they saw something and asked about it. My instinct would be to tell some story about hurting myself. But I doubt either of them would believe me anyway. I can't convincingly lie to anyone, let alone my best friends.

And then, there's what Max expects me to say. *I don't think I could do it.* I think I would die at the age of 26 from the heatstroke of that much embarrassment if I had to say those words to them. Tracy would probably die of shock.

I'd have to tell them something, though. And the sinking feeling in my stomach, the knot that has made me only choke down a few bites of my sandwich, is that I know I'd tell them the truth, a version of the truth anyway. That Max and I had an argument and he slapped me. I can feel my face turning red as I think this. But this isn't even the truth. If I tell the truth,F it's that I was bad and Max punished me...*just like he warned me he would. But I can't say that*! I'd say the partial-true version...*maybe.*

I'd have to. Otherwise, if they saw Max and made some comment about a story I made up; he'd be mad and I'd be in trouble. *Not an option.* Better to deal with my friends than Max.

I only feel more red and sick with this self-realization. I'd choose Max not being mad at me over keeping the peace with my friends. Max would probably still be a little upset, because I know that I wouldn't be able to tell them everything. *But he wouldn't be mad at me for telling a complete lie at least.*

"Hey...you okay? Are you still not feeling well?" Tracy is looking a little too closely at me. I realize I've been quiet and thinking my own thoughts for too long. She's referring to my calling in sick yesterday. She and Laura had both sent texts that they could come over after work and take care of me. I texted back that I was only feeling a little badly, mostly playing hooky with Max.

I made sure they sat together in the booth opposite me, so I could keep my head down. I lower my face more, like I'm going to take a big bite of my sandwich, "I'm fine...just a long day already. Cruela is really riding everyone since the interviews haven't panned out lately." Tracy and Laura both know that their own marketing team has two open positions that we've had a hard time filling. My boss has been under fire for not being able to get the right candidates to stay in positions for more than a year. Not the candidates that I've placed, but she isn't discriminating in her broom-riding tirades.

"Well...you and Kevin have been her only bright spots. The most trouble seems to be in the accounting positions anyway. She should lighten up on you." Tracy sits back. Laura keeps watching me though. I take a bite of sandwich from the side, so my face is more away from her again. She finally looks away.

"So are we still on for tomorrow?" Tracy changes the subject. I almost groan out loud, but stop myself and look down quickly to hide my reaction.

"Tad and I'll bring beer and popcorn." Laura is excited about the plans we made last Friday. When we were out for our girls-only night of dancing, I'd agreed to a Saturday movie night at Tracy's this weekend.

So much has changed in only one week. I completely forgot about making these plans, but I cover it, "We'll bring wine."

"Great. Josh and I'll have pizzas delivered. This'll be fun." She and Josh, her on-off boyfriend, have been more on than off lately. She doesn't want to admit that since their last breakup over three months ago, she's been more into him. Laura and I share an eye roll and laugh. It feels good to laugh with them again.

During my next interview, though, I'm completely distracted. I realize that I not only forgot about making the plans, I haven't told Max about them.

Since he slapped me because I was cursing along with Tracy and Laura, I'm afraid of how he'll react to my suggestion that we spend tomorrow night with them. I am relieved, though, that I didn't have to tell any stories, half-truths, or truths over lunch.

I touch my cheek. I know why Max wanted to leave his mark on me. *I've certainly been able to think of nothing else for a while.* It doesn't hurt, just looks a little bad. I still can't believe how much is changed by this. *When I look in the mirror... I know that I belong to him...that I will never be the same again. I've let him punish me...*

3 Him

I smile. I can see Lucy waiting on the sidewalk outside her building. I'm early. My smile falters though when I see that Tracy is waiting with her.

Tracy is what I call a 'bad influence.' Lucy admitted that her own mom believes Tracy contributes to her having a more foul mouth than she should. And I've seen for myself how Lucy behaves more boldly around this friend. It's why she was cursing the other night. *Hopefully, Lucy is broken of that habit.* I grin, *if not, she'll be a very sorry little girl again in the future.*

Jeff opens the door for Lucy and she gets in. Tracy leans in before the door closes. "So I'll see you guys tomorrow at 7:00. Don't forget the wine!" She slams the car door before Jeff can move in her way. Lucy doesn't look at me. She looks everywhere but at me.

I let her squirm a little longer. She fidgets with her purse, taking out a mirror and pretending to check her makeup. I can tell she's already reapplied before waiting for me. She adds more powder anyway.

"What was that about?" I put my hand on her knee. She kicks her leg up in response, but doesn't laugh at my ticklish squeeze.

"Um...I forgot..." she darts looks at me, then at Jeff in the front seat, then back at me, "...to mention that I made plans for us to do a movie night tomorrow..." more darting, and she swallows, "...at Tracy's."

I've been texting her all day. She said her friends and co-workers hadn't noticed anything. She was fine. She didn't say anything about this until now.

"Ask me."

Her head whips sideways to face me; she holds her makeup in the air in front of her. I smile at the look of shock and shame on her.

"I..." She stops, lowering her makeup and hands to her lap. I see a cloud of emotions fight over control of her face. She turns to me, "...I made plans for us..." She tries to say this with a strong voice, but she squeaks at the end. It's more a plea than a statement. I raise an eyebrow in response. She lowers her eyes.

"Oh...?" I smile as she lowers her chin slightly as I drip sarcasm into this simple accusation. "Is that how you *ask* me, Lucy?" I've been nervous about her facing her friends and co-workers all day, about how she'd react if they commented on anything. I wondered if she'd be able to withstand outside influences in how our relationship is developing. It's why I left a mark on her that is so visible...*I need to know that she's mine...no matter what anybody says to her.*

I've been hopeful in her text responses, but now is the real test. I need to push her, again. *I need to put her in her place and keep her there.* I allow myself a small smile while her eyes are still lowered.

I wait for her to finally raise her eyes to me, her chin still lowered, "Can we go to Tracy's tomorrow night, Max?" She asks in such a sweet little voice.

"You don't have the *right* to decide what *you* do, what *we* do, anymore. I expect you not to make plans again, Lucy. You get my permission *first*. Do you understand me?" I continue my hard look at her, ignoring her question for a moment, taking this golden opportunity to drive home the message that she's no longer in control of herself, her life.

She shrinks into the seat more, fidgeting her fingers together in her dress, looking furtively at Jeff to see if he can hear us. "Yes, Sir...I won't," her answer is tiny.

"Good." I continue staring at her for another moment. Her cheeks are blooming with the heat of her embarrassment, her eyes a bright blue and wide, and her tits heave nicely in the form-fitting dress. I'm proud of her for not asking me for an answer. "We can go tomorrow."

She's so tightly wound that she jumps into my arms and kisses me at the release of her tension, "Thank you, Max!"

"You just better be on your best behavior." She squeezes me more and promises to be.

4 Her

I'm nervous. I keep checking myself in the mirror. My makeup has stayed on well; but then again, I've reapplied three times today. Max finally tells me to put the mirror away.

I would rather be heading home for an early night with Max, than out to dinner with his friends. Today has been exhausting. But I know better than to make this suggestion to him. He would definitely not be happy with me questioning his plans. *And he did just agree to go to Tracy's tomorrow...but that might just be even more stress for me.*

We arrive at the restaurant and I smile to myself while I wait for Jeff to open my door...*pet-peeve avoided.* I don't know who is going to be here tonight. I imagine that it will be the friends that I've met of his, Dan and Becca, Mike and Stephie. I like all of them. Stephie was rude at first, but now she's sweet to me. Mike is a goof ball and makes me laugh a lot, something I could use tonight. And Dan acts like an older brother to Max, with Becca acting like a mother hen to the whole group, so both were welcoming to me from the start.

Max is waiting for me on the sidewalk. His tall, dark looks excite me. In a white shirt over light linen pants, his strong muscles and lean body are on display nicely. He looks so perfectly casual, yet carries himself like he's in a full suit. Two women walking into the restaurant try to catch his eye, but he only looks at me as I walk to him. He kisses my cheek and presses me to his side, "Have I told you how beautiful you are tonight?" I blush. He says he loves this about me, how easily I blush and show my emotions.

"Only a few times..." My smile feels great; I relax a little more, sending much needed relief to my knotted stomach.

"My brother's going to love you." He is already opening the door, before this sinks in.

"Your brother's here?" He doesn't answer, just continues to lead me inside. The lobby area is full of people waiting for tables already. We head towards the large bar in the back. Max stops, though, to look at his phone.

"Sorry, baby, I have to take this. Wait for me in the bar." He turns to head back outside to hear better.

I hesitate, in a limbo of emotions. The knot is back in my stomach. I know that I have to walk into the bar. Max told me to wait for him there. If I don't, he'll be upset with me. But I'm scared to walk in there and meet his brother without him.

I stay still for a moment longer, calming myself with what I do know already about his brother. Jake is 32, three years younger than Max, and lives in Old Town with his girlfriend, can't remember her name. Jake didn't follow the path set by their dad; he didn't become a lawyer like Max did; he didn't join the family firm like Max did. He also didn't take the brunt of the abuse from their mom when they were younger, because Max protected him as much as he could. The abuse stopped when Ron married their mom and adopted them both.

I take a deep breath. *Better head in.*

I see Dan before anyone else. He's almost the same height as Max and stands out in a crowd. I make my way towards him and he waves as he sees me. "Where's Max?"

"He's right outside. Had to take a call first." I look around. I only see Becca and Stephie sitting at the bar. *Phew*.

"Here. I got an extra one since it's happy hour prices. I thought Mike would be here by now." Stephie hands me a glass from in front of her. It's gin and tonic, not my favorite. But I could really use a drink about now. I take a big gulp before thanking her.

"How's your gallery opening going?" Becca takes a gulp of her drink too before answering me.

"Great. I think I've got a place lined up in River North. It's this cool loft gallery that hosts up-and-coming exhibits along with their rotating regular pieces. It's one of my favorites for finding hidden gems for my clients. I just hope another art broker thinks my art is a gem now for someone else."

"You'll do great. You do great at everything." Stephie shakes her shoulder and I nod in support.

Dan adds, "I think she's underpricing herself...but she's the expert."

Becca slaps his stomach, but is smiling, "Thank you, supportive husband."

I realize that I've downed almost all the drink and start to put it on the bar to avoid drinking the rest. Max puts his hand on my shoulder and I turn towards him in a quick startled motion. Dan is the first to greet him, though, "Hey, the conquering hero has arrived! Congrats on closing that deal today with Hoffman. That place is going to be great for the LPE Group."

"Thanks." He takes Dan's outstretched hand and shakes it. Then he takes the drink from my hand and I can tell he's upset. At first I can't tell if it's at me or from his call. His look darkens and by the strange electrical pulse that runs from my stomach down to my pussy, I know it's me. I'm just not sure what it is that I've done to upset him though. My stomach knots more watching him watch me.

He glances down at the drink now in his hand and finishes it. Leaning over me to put it on the bar. He gets the attention of the bartender and orders two glasses of wine for us.

I try to lighten his mood, kissing his cheek as he leans over me, "You didn't tell me...Congrats, Max." He works for his dad at the firm, but he mostly works for himself, as a silent partner and attorney for the Lincoln Park Entertainment Group. It's one of the largest owner/management groups of restaurants and bars in the city. *He doesn't really talk business with me, though. He doesn't even ask about my job.*

Max ignores me and answers Dan instead, "You're just happy because it means I'm always going to be able to get us a table at one of your favorite spots in town now." Max is laughing, but the dark look hasn't left his eyes. He keeps flicking them at me.

"You wound me, friend." Dan is clapping his back though and everyone's laughing. I join in, but only for a second.

The bartender hands our wine to Max. He hands me one, but doesn't let go. He leans over my side, "That's strike one, little girl." I swallow and feel my face turning red. He didn't whisper it, just said it in his usual deep voice. I glance around to see if anyone heard him. He nods at me and lets me take the glass. *He must be upset that I had that drink before he arrived.* It's his biggest pet-peeve so far. He always orders everything for me. It's been this way since we met, and I've never challenged him on it.

It's one of the strangest parts of our relationship. From the beginning, Max has been more attentive than any other guy I've dated. He notices everything, keeps an eye on me at all times when we're together, and always does little things to show me how special I am to him. But his attentiveness also means he has a lot of these pet-peeves, a long list of things he does or doesn't want me to do. I don't have to guess how to make him happy. He tells, shows me.

And I have surprised myself with how much I like it this way. He's in control. There's never been a question about this in my mind. *Take Max, take his control.* It wasn't until after our trip to meet his parents though that I realized how deep this need for control goes. *His. And mine.*

I've never really liked the wishy-washy nature of guys I've dated before, leaving everything up to me to decide, leaving the brunt of relationship building and commitment pushing up to me. Max has been different from the start. And the depth of my response to him has surprised me.

I've wanted to please him from the beginning. I've wanted to follow his little rules and old-fashion-ness to show him how much he means to me. I've been proud of being able to do every little thing he's asked. Since he slapped me, though, there's also been this element of fear of not pleasing him.

And the depth of my response to that has been the hardest for me to understand. Just looking at the darkened look he still wears now...*I'm wet. He made me a promise. And I know that I can trust him. I know that I can give into these feelings...that I'm safe...to be turned on by his anger, his control.*

5 Him

I like watching her change before my eyes. She shrinks into herself, blushes, looks around embarrassed. She's aware that I'm angry with her and she's trying to figure out why. She should know by now, though. *I'll have to make that lesson more memorable for her.* I keep an eye on her, admiring how beautiful her blue eyes look when they are tinged with fear.

Dan is asking Stephie about her latest case, "...So is the defendant as sleaze-bag as the blogs make him out to be?" Since attending law school with Dan, Mike, and Stephie, Stephie has been the only one of us who has stayed in her original field, civil defense.

She puts on her best "lawyer face for the cameras" as we called it at Northwestern, "I cannot confirm nor deny these allegations, gentle sir." We laugh, but I like seeing that Lucy is still too on edge to laugh much.

Before Dan can give a smartass comment back, Jake arrives and hugs everyone, stopping in front of me. "You must be Lucy?" He smiles down at her from the same height as me. We could almost be twins, except he keeps his wavy brown hair longer, touching his collar.

She gives him one of her prettiest smiles, with her head held back and eyes sparkling. "You must be Jake?" They shake hands.

Stephie breaks in though, reaching with her hand towards Lucy's jaw, "Oh, honey, you have a little smudge."

Lucy moves her head down quickly to cover the bruise with her hair again, but not before seeing the accusing look Jake shoots at me. Stephie doesn't notice anything and goes back to teasing Dan.

Lucy remains with her head down, her eyes turned pleadingly up at me. Jake turns to face me more and looks like he's going to say something. I only smile calmly at my brother's clenched jaw.

"Here you are! I looked around the restaurant for you since I'm so late." Jake's girlfriend interrupts his glare. He relaxes his face and returns her hug, taking his eyes off of me.

"Hi, Julia." I give her a hug in return too and turn her towards Lucy, "Lucy, Julia."

"Nice to meet you." both girls say in unison, shaking hands. Lucy's laugh is shaky and shy. I put my arm around her and pull her to my side firmly.

Mike arrives within seconds, "Sorry I'm late. Had to get across town in the Friday rush." He slides in to stand next to Stephie.

She kisses him, but says, "I gave your drink away...serves ya right!" Dan and Becca laugh at this, but Lucy only buries her head more in my side. *Good girl.*

Jake sits across the long table from me. His eyes keep travelling from me to Lucy. His jaw is no longer clenched though. His look is more questioning, his brow pulled down. I return his stare calmly, keeping my face neutral.

Lucy remains with her hands in her lap, not picking up the menu in front of her. I put my hand on her knee and she grabs it with both of hers like a lifesaver.

Stephie turns to Lucy suddenly, "Hey...Lucy, we never got what you do for a living?"

"I...I'm in human resources," Lucy is thrown off by the sudden spotlight again. "I'm in recruiting."

"My lucky day! Maybe you could help me then?" Julia leans over her menu across the table. "I could *really* use some interviewing pointers." She tells everybody that she's trying for a promotion, but has to interview for the job since it's with a different division.

"Yeah, Max. You'd like that wouldn't you? *Your* girlfriend helping mine to get ahead in the business world?" Jake says this quietly, but with enough sarcasm to make Julia look at him curiously.

Lucy answers before I can, "I'd love to help."

"Great. Maybe over lunch next week...my treat?" Julia sits back. She smiles at Lucy, but still has a frown at the looks Jake and I are exchanging.

"Sounds good," Lucy answers quietly, also responding to the tension between us.

"How's your little *business* going, Jake?" I take a drink of wine, still calmly meeting my brother's stare. He clenches his jaw again.

Dan interrupts, "I heard you got a city contract to make over the old Union Building? Congrats, Jake." Dan gives me his "be cool" look, his eyes wide, brows raised, head nodding, raising a glass in Jake's direction. Big brother trying to make peace. Both Mike and Dan are aware of our family rift.

Mike joins in the peacekeeping effort, "Yeah, that's a big deal. Congrats." He raises his glass for everyone to cheer. I join in, but don't clink glasses with Jake. He pulls his glass away from mine too.

The waitress arrives and stops next to my chair, "Hello, Mr. Traeger. It's so nice to see you. Do you remember me? I worked at Frogs Leap as a hostess." I try to remember all the employees I come in contact with at the LPE restaurants. It's a very incestuous business and it's important to put names with faces quickly when making decisions about staff.

"Of course. Veronica. It's great to see you too."

"And thanks for the recommendation. It made getting this job super easy." She had been a good employee, but we closed the place down for four months of renovations last year and let everyone go.

"I'm glad. Let me know if you're ever looking to make a move back, we have an opening in parties and catering..." I know this is one of the areas that all wait staff love, better pay, bigger tips, and less hours. She'd be perfect since she already knows most of the menu and the catering manager.

Her smile gets bigger. "I'll think about it. Thank you." She turns to the rest of the table, "Some of you look set on drinks; I'll get orders for those who aren't. But does anyone have any questions on the menu so far?"

Jake speaks up, "Lucy...do you have a question? You've hardly looked at your menu..." He's staring pointedly at me again.

Veronica starts to turn to Lucy, but I answer, also staring at Jake, "She's fine." He bows his head sarcastically to me.

Mike breaks the tension. "Actually...I think we could use more drinks all around, Veronica." Stephie and Becca gulp down the last of their drinks and hand the empties to Veronica. She doesn't miss a beat. Jake finally stops glaring at me when it's his turn to order.

The rest have left already, leaving Jake and me alone. Dan squeezed my shoulder on his way out and said, "Play nice, boys." Giving Jake a nod as good-bye. Lucy and Julia excused themselves to the bathroom shortly after.

Jake doesn't waste any time, as soon as we're alone, "I can't believe you!" He's staring at me, leaning forward, his hands open on the cleared table. I only look at him, waiting for him to continue. He was always more emotional than me. "You're *really* following in Ron's footsteps now, aren't you?" He's trying for sarcastic, but it comes across as more of an actual question.

"Our *father* is a good man, Jake. Careful how you speak about him." I lower my voice, speak slowly, and give him The Look. It's what we called the expression that came over our dad's face when we did something wrong. It's a brows furrowed, jaw clenched, eyes piercing look. We always knew we were in trouble when we got it.

Jake is my little brother. I've always protected him. *But I am not going to take shit off of him.* He's always responded to me, backing off when I really push him. He leans back in his chair, taking a deep breath. "Look, Max..." He runs his hand through his waves, and leans forward into the table once more. Lowering his voice to almost a whisper, "I can tell that you really like this girl...and she's obviously crazy about you..." He falters when I sigh and frown more.

"I love her. And she loves me." I can see that he's surprised at my matter-of-fact tone in making this statement about a girl that he hasn't even met before.

He shakes his head in response, "But, you don't have to go down this path..." He shrugs at the end. Lucy and Julia are returning to the table, so he says no more. He stands up before either of them can sit back down. I stand up too.

But I wait until short good-byes are given, before grabbing Lucy in a hug. "You were a very good girl tonight." She beams a smile up at me. "Except for that one slip...we'll have to address that later." The pretty shift from disappoint, fear, and anxious need to please that plays across her face makes me smile and kiss her again. "Let's go. It's been a long day, baby."

In the car, Lucy falls asleep with her head on my shoulder. *Poor, girl...she has had a long day. The beginning to all the rest of our days together.*

I still can't believe how quickly everything's progressed with Lucy. We've only known each other a little over a month, and I'm already comfortable being myself with her. No keeping a distance, like with the girls I took on random dates to events and just for sex. No hiding what I believe until I think the moment is right to try for something more meaningful, like with past girlfriends. No pretending that a girl who only submits to my demands in the bedroom is good enough for me, like past unsuccessful relationships.

I don't remember making a conscious decision to be different with her, but with Lucy, everything *has* been different. From the beginning, I've been controlling and demanding. And she's responded perfectly, in sync with how I think and feel...*how I believe it should be between me and mine.*

I know Jake rejects how we were raised. It's because he doesn't remember how bad it was before Ron came along. How bad *Mom* was before him. *But I do.*

The first seven years of my life were crap. My dad was a deadbeat, never marrying my under aged mom, dragging her into his seedy drugged-up life, disappearing a year after fathering my brother. My mom was overwhelmed, unable to cope with what life had handed her. Until she met Ron. He turned everything around in one night.

He stopped her from beating my brother for something minor. I overheard it all. I'd crept out of our bedroom while Jake stayed cowering and crying in his bed. I heard Ron yell at my mom. And I heard him spank her. She'd begged, cried, tried to get away even. I heard him beat her with his belt that night.

The next day, he sat Jake and me at the kitchen table and explained that he was going to be our dad from then on. That he was going to be in charge and things would be different around the house. Our mom only smiled and looked down at her hand on his shoulder the whole time.

I also remember that she didn't sit down for almost a week...just like I didn't when she took Jake's punishment out on me the year before. But then she'd used her fist and my back was too sore to sit that long.

Remembering this doesn't make me bitter or angry. I know that my mom is a good woman now. She's loving, caring, considerate, kind. She's everything that a wife and mother should be. All thanks to Ron. His tough-love showed her how to be a good woman.

Jake doesn't understand this though. We talked before I went to college. He said he was afraid to be left alone with Ron's anger. I told him that Ron's anger served a purpose, to help us to be better people, that he had nothing to fear.

But I know that he never saw it this way. He doesn't remember Mom's anger, her violence. He only remembers how strict, controlling, and disciplinarian Ron was to all of us. He thinks that Mom could've been a good mother on her own...*I know he's wrong.*

I only hope that there's enough of Ron in me to counterbalance my own anger issues...

6 Her

I wake to the sound of Max talking from his living room. I can't hear what he's saying, but his tone is dangerously close to angry. We didn't talk when we got home. I was too exhausted and he said we could discuss everything that happened yesterday in the morning.

I don't think I've ever slept so soundly. The last several days have been emotionally and physically exhausting. I feel more relaxed and myself this morning. But his voice is putting me on edge again. Curiosity gets to me and I climb out of bed. Grabbing the t-shirt of his I wore two days before, I head towards the kitchen.

Just in the hall, his words come clear, "You don't have anything figured out! You think you can just turn your back and bam...become a different person? It's not that simple!"

I see him standing with one hand on his hip, in front of the floor-to-ceiling windows. The top-floor view of the city hardscape spans beyond him. His back muscles are tense, looking like a sculpture of a beautiful angry god ready to strike down the city below his feet.

I don't interrupt him, just turn into the kitchen and pour coffee as quietly as I can into the mug he left for me. I'm still not sure who he is talking to or what about.

"He taught us well. You think doing just the opposite of what he wants for you is going to make you a *better* person, little brother?" *So he's talking to Jake.* I swallow the hot coffee down hard. I want to slip back into the bedroom and pretend I haven't heard anything, but I know I can't do this. I stay in the kitchen out of sight.

"I *am* a better person! I've lived my life exactly how *I* want. And with Lucy, I *have* exactly what I want." He doesn't pause long to let Jake say anything. "You think *living* with a girl, pretending that you're okay with Julia's ambitions, putting you on the backburner all these years...you *really* want to tell me that you're okay with that?" He's almost yelling into the phone. But he pauses to allow Jake to speak this time.

His voice is quieter when he answers, "I don't believe you, Jake...I know you. And I know that you want more than that for yourself..." There's a long pause again. "You haven't even been honest with Julia...Mom and Dad haven't even met her." The pause stretches. "I *am* honest with Lucy. She knows exactly who and what I am."

His voice is deadly deep, the chill to whatever his brother has said making me shiver at hearing him. I'm shrinking back against the cabinets, holding the mug up close under my chin, breathing in the warm coffee goodness and praying that he'll be off the phone soon. I don't want to hear him discussing me with his brother.

"You don't get it...I've never *lied* to her. Lucy knows her place." The pause is short. I'm holding my breath as he quickly continues, obviously talking over Jake, "You *are* lying to Julia. By not being honest with who you are!" He stops. I can hear him taking a deep breath to calm himself. "You think warning Lucy against me will make a difference...then go ahead, *little* brother." I can't tell if he's hung up or is just letting Jake rant.

He hasn't moved. I'm sick with what I overheard. *Jake knows what has happened between us...and he wants to warn me about something...I just want to crawl back into bed...*

I look up and Max is standing in the doorway. He was so quiet I didn't hear him move. The phone is still in his hand, now at his side. The look on his face is dark only for a moment. His eyes clear as if a strong wind has blown away the shadow hanging over his brow.

"Good morning." He doesn't move though. So I go to him. I slip my arms around his middle and squeeze. He breathes in my hair and kisses my head.

"You heard some of that?" He's not really asking if I heard just how much of it.

"Yes...you were talking to Jake?" I don't really want to talk to him about this. It brings up the stress of yesterday, of his brother's reaction to Stephie mistaking the bruise for something else on my jaw. I look down at my feet.

"Yes. He wanted to confront me about you. Well, more than he did last night anyway." Max sighs heavily, rubbing my back. "Jake thinks he has things figured out that he really has no idea about." Max sounds so sad, so resigned. I look up into his face and see the sadness there. I reach up and touch his cheek gently. He looks down at me and smiles, "Jake thinks living with his girlfriend, letting her run the show, not seeing our parents, and talking shit to his big brother, means that he's grown up....he has no idea how far off he is." He kisses my head and swats my butt. "Make breakfast, Lucy."

His abrupt change to a command surprises me. It falters me into asking, "So what does he want to warn *me* about?" I stay frozen in place, watching him.

Max stops in his turn towards the coffee machine, but only for a second. He doesn't answer, just pours himself more coffee, taking his time adding some creamer and stirring. I can see his back tensing though, his shoulders rounding, muscles flexing. He doesn't turn to me, "I told you to do something, didn't I?"

It's a soft, edgy, voice. A warning voice. And I respond in an instant. I move to the cabinet under the stove where he keeps his pans. "Would you like eggs, sweetie?" My voice is artificially elevated, made higher by my fear.

"No." He turns to me now, leaning against his cabinet, still stirring his mug. "*Ask* me what I'd like."

I freeze, the frying pan hanging mid-air above the stove. "Oh..." the wind is knocked out of my lungs. "What would you like to eat?" It's all monosyllable, numb.

I still hold the pan in my hand as he answers. "I'll have two pieces of French toast and an over easy egg." He steps towards me and kisses my cheek. "You'll have an over easy egg and one piece of toast...*not* burnt." He tilts my chin up and raises an eyebrow to me, before finishing with a kiss. "We're taking a shower first, so you can start breakfast after." He pulls my hand behind him toward the hallway.

This is different. He's demanding, controlling, as usual...but somehow different...no question about my obedience to his exact demands... I move in a state of numbness. *And wetness.* I barely have time to put the pan on a counter as I follow him.

I am just finishing the eggs, adding everything to a plate when a buzzer sounds. I jump. My hair is in damp ringlets over the same t-shirt. I have my thong on too but nothing else. Max wouldn't let me get dressed before making his breakfast.

I watch as Max moves in his tan shorts and green short-sleeve shirt towards the front door. I continue putting breakfast together. *I have everything just as he asked.* I smile. I even added sliced oranges to the plates.

He was rough in the shower. Pushing soapy fingers into my pussy and shoving me hard against the shower walls. I thought he might slap me again, but he only pushed me around and fucked me hard. I'm still pulsing from it.

I freeze when I hear Jake's voice. He follows just behind Max into the kitchen. Max smiles at me, "Get a cup of coffee for my brother, baby."

I am already putting a plate down and turning towards where Max keeps cups, when Jake stops me. He looks embarrassed and doesn't make eye contact with me. "No...No need, really....I didn't realize that you weren't alone, Max." He lifts his eyes to stare into the bright green of Max's.

"Lucy already overhead our conversation from before..." Max is taking a bite of French toast from his plate, looking between Jake and me. "She knows you have something to say to her. Why don't you just say it..." he chews loudly, taking a napkin and wiping his mouth. He smiles at me, then Jake. Jake looks to me, then Max.

"How bout I leave you two alone..." To my surprise, Max takes his plate and walks out to the terrace, leaving me in the kitchen with Jake.

I put my plate down on the counter with a loud clank. "Say what you want to say...get this over with, *please*!" My nerves are shot from so many days in stress mode.

Jake only looks at me with such tenderness, that I almost cry. "How are you doing, Lucy?" His voice reminds me of Max, strong, deep, urging, but without the edge of angry.

"I'm fine." I take a bite of my toast defensively.

"Can I see your face?" He almost whispers this, so tender.

I can't swallow my bite for a minute, "...Why...?" I know it's a stupid question, but I'm stalling now. I glance at the terrace. Max is sitting with his back to us. I didn't put any makeup on after our shower. The bruises are fading, but still clearly visible.

"Because I want to see what he did to you," Jake almost whispers.

I stare into his eyes for what feels like a long time. I notice that his eyes are more of an emerald green to Max's pale pond green. He doesn't blink; neither do I. His look remains soft, sweet even. I remain numb, questioning at best, brows narrowed, mouth twisted.

I finally put my fork down with a loud clang and pull my hair back defiantly from the left side of my face with one hand. "There. Now you saw." I drop my hair, but keep my face turned to the right to hide the marks. My defiance ran out of steam quickly.

Jake moves slowly towards me with his hand outstretched. I'm shocked, but watch as he comes closer to me. I wouldn't dream of letting another man touch me, not in this apartment, not with Max this close, not ever. Yet, I stand still while Jake puts his hand on my shoulder and runs it up the side of my neck to stop in my hair, rubbing my head briefly before quickly pulling his hand away.

He only repeats himself, "Are you okay?" with a stronger voice, more emotion hidden in the gravel.

I look up at him, my eyes burning with tears. Humiliation, desire to please Max, and fear making my own voice stop in my throat. Finally, I find the breath to speak again, "...you wanted to tell me something...?"

Jake doesn't move away from me. He towers over me, just like Max. "I wanted to tell you that Max..." He turns away, looking out towards the terrace for a second. "I know he loves you..." He keeps starting and stopping, unsure of himself. *So different from his brother.*

I reach for his shoulder, but stop myself and quickly pull my hand back looking guiltily outside. Jake starts again, turning back to me. "Our dad...he was a cruel man sometimes. He loved us. All of us. But..." He shakes his head, takes in a shaky breath, "But he wasn't always *loving* to us...to our mom. There were many mornings that I found her crying, hiding what he had done." He looks pointedly at me. "Days when she wouldn't come out of their room...when he wouldn't *let* her." He raises his arm towards Max, "And *he* thinks it was all okay. That we had a great childhood." He lowers his arm, shaking his head again. "You've met my mom. She's a sweet, caring person, but she allowed our dad to push her around..."

I interrupt him, but my voice sounds far away to me, "Max said...He said your mom wasn't always..." I don't want to repeat the abuse Max said he suffered as a young boy. "That you were too young to remember...that he protected you..."

Jake's smile is twisted, a grimace, "Yeah. He's told me that too...but I...I can't believe that that's the truth..." He stands taller, squaring his shoulders more. "And you shouldn't believe it either, Lucy." He puts his hands on my shoulders, scaring me again with his closeness. I dart my eyes to the terrace. Max still has his back to us. I keep my eyes on Max. Jake sees my fear and quickly drops his hands and takes a step back. "I don't want you to get hurt, Lucy, because *he* thinks it's the only way to love." He adds, softly, "You deserve better than that..."

I dart my eyes back to Jake at this. "How do you know what I deserve? You don't know me, Jake." I have a little defiance, a little anger in me at being put in this humiliating situation by him. But I finish with almost a plea, "You don't know anything about me..."

"You're right..." He puts his hands up, "I don't know you. But I do know Max. And he'll do exactly what our dad did. He'll follow in his footsteps like a good little soldier." He puts his hands in his pockets. "He'll change you into exactly what he wants." Max is walking back in. "Is that what *you* really want, Lucy?" Jakes finishes quickly.

"Time's up, little brother," Max stands in the doorway, looking only at Jake. I just look from one to the other, almost mirror images, same clenched jaws, tight faces, piercing eyes. "Did you say your piece?"

Jake looks at me, face still set, "Yeah…" He turns to walk down the hallway to the door, Max following him.

"Wait!" Both men turn, startled, to me. "You didn't get my answer…" Same mirrored response, both faces morphed into surprise, eyebrows up. "Yes."

Jake only shakes his head and turns to leave. Max continues looking at me, searching my face; finally, he smiles and turns towards the door just as Jake shuts it. He stands with his back to me for a moment.

I walk to the bedroom quickly, tears welling up. I slam the bathroom door shut and lean over the counter, crying. The door bangs open a moment later and I jump, crying out, hand to my mouth. Max comes in, but doesn't move towards me, just stares at me with his eyes narrow. "Wanna tell me what you think you're doing?" The edge is back in his voice, cutting into the air between us.

"I…I just need a minute…" I sniffle, wiping my cheeks with flat hands.

"So you think that makes it okay for you to slam a door? To even *shut* a door on me?" He hasn't moved, but stands taller, shoulders filling the whole frame. There's no way to get around him.

"I…I'm sorry, Max…" I'd forgotten this rule in my panic.

His shoulders relax slightly, "You're just lucky that you didn't try to lock it." He walks further into the room, standing in front of me. He puts both hands on the sides of my face and wipes my tears with his thumbs, smiling as I flinched when he raised his hands. He stares into my eyes for a moment longer, then kisses my forehead and lowers his hands. He turns to leave.

"Max…this wasn't fair…" I can't stop myself. The chaos of emotions in me bubbles to the surface and I can't breathe. I start to shake, tears falling again. "You shouldn't have left me alone with him…"

Max turns back slowly. I shrink away in anticipation of the anger I expect to see. Max only looks hurt, sad. And my reaction is instant. I jump towards him, into his arms, slamming myself against his chest. He holds my back and my head, hands rubbing my hair. "Shhh…It's okay, baby. It's going to be okay."

We stay like this for a while, until my breathing calms. Finally, he answers me, "I told you that you need to be able to stand up for us, for yourself in this. Jake isn't the only one who is going to question how things are between us." He pulls back to look at my face.

The dawning panic he sees makes him continue, "Lucy…what we have isn't for everyone…and you have to expect that some people will try to butt into our business." He pauses, watching me; I only nod. He lifts my chin, "I expect you to be able to hold your head up and stand by my side no matter what."

I don't move, forcing my breathing to even out again, my chin still in his hand. "You did just fine with Jake." He kisses my nose. I manage a small smile and he lets go of my chin. "What were you saying yes to?"

He's watching me again. "He said you would change me." I look directly into his eyes. "And I said that's what I want." He smiles brightly at me; I snuggle into his arms again. I feel safe and calm once more.

7 Him

Before walking up the final set of stairs, I pull Lucy back for a deep kiss. She responds as always, melting into me, fingers wrapped in my hair.

After this morning with Jake, she's been quieter, moving around the apartment in tiny, tentative movements. I know she needs a lot of reassurance.

She smiles, her biggest smile today, hands dangling over my shoulders. "Are you ready to hang out with *my* friends tonight?" I don't like being here, but I think being around her friends will help her to feel better. *And it's a step we need to take.*

"Yes, as long as you behave yourself." I wink at her though. I haven't pushed her since this morning. But that doesn't mean I'm going to let her get away with acting up tonight.

Her smile gets even bigger for a moment, "Of course."
I'm hopeful that her moodiness is gone because my patience
is.

The door opens. It's Laura answering, hugging Lucy
and welcoming me. She takes the bottles of wine we brought
into the small kitchen and I follow her to open them.

Josh is stretched out on the sofa; Tad's in an oversized
chair. The large flat screen is on, but paused. The smell of
popcorn is strong. Lucy has already moved into the other
oversized chair. I don't see Tracy anywhere. *I'm going to try
to be as nice to that girl as I can tonight.* It is her apartment
after all, but her foul mouth, loud ways get on my nerves
quickly.

Laura and I return to the living room, putting the two
bottles down next to the assortment of wine glasses on the
coffee table.

"You look nice, all dressed up for us." Tracy kicks
Josh's feet out of her way and stops next to Lucy, putting her
phone on the coffee table.

Lucy looks just the way I like her to, sweet. Hair down
and more to the left still, she's wearing a flowy long dress,
with a cropped short-sleeve sweater over it and one button
done to cover her cleavage more. She had tried to wear
shorts tonight. I think she thought she could get away with it,
since I was being more indulgent with her today. She
quickly changed with only the slightest warning in my look
to her.

"Thanks." She's smiling up at me. I sit, pulling her
back with me, my arm around her. "And you guys all
look…um, *nice*." She's laughing, since everyone else is in

baggy t-shirts and shorts. Josh doesn't even have matching socks on.

Tracy sits down and flips her middle finger towards us with a sarcastic grin. *She's a gem of a girl.* Lucy only lowers her head and tries not to look at me. She knows I'm not smiling.

Tracy sits back into Josh and starts the movie. It's the latest in a vampire series, not in theaters long. Laura gets up and hands us a bowl of popcorn of our own. She's a sweet girl. I think she could do better than Tad. He's nice, but not very driven.

After only thirty minutes, Tracy's phone vibrates on the table. She picks up the call, "Okay. Be right down." She turns to Josh, "Pizza's here."

He only shakes his head, "No. I went last time. Your turn."

Tad asks, "Why don't you just buzz the guy in?"

Tracy answers, "Because the little old lady on the second floor was punched and robbed last month and made everyone in the building *promise* not to let any delivery people in anymore *unattended* as she put it." She pushes Josh's shoulder. "You go." But Josh only crosses his arms and shakes his head.

"A girl really shouldn't answer the door this late alone," I stand up and leave the apartment.

When I return with the pizzas, Laura is sitting next to Tracy on the sofa and Lucy is still sitting in the chair, fidgeting with her hands. They all just look up at me, not saying anything. I walk into the kitchen and set the pizzas down. Tad and Josh are drinking beer in here. Josh glares at me.

Tad looks sheepish, "The money's over there." He points with his bottle towards a few bills sitting on the counter. I don't move, just stare back at Josh.

He pushes himself off the counter to address me finally, "Man… You don't have to come in here and I dunno know…act like you're better than everyone."

"Sorry if I stepped on your toes, Josh," but I keep my voice even, no apology in it, facing him directly.

Tracy comes into the kitchen and pushes by me. Taking Josh's arm, she pulls him a little and he looks at her. "Can you get us two pieces and come back to watch the movie now?" She doesn't wait for his answer, just pushes by me again.

I return to sitting with Lucy. Tad and Josh come in with plates and take their seats. Laura jumps up to be next to Tad again. Tracy starts the movie, but keeps some distance from Josh now.

Lucy whispers to me, "Do you want some pizza?"

I smile, brushing her hair away from her face and kiss her. "Thanks, baby." She jumps up and returns quickly with plates for us.

Another half hour goes by before Tracy finally thaws towards Josh again. Laura and Lucy both relax, then. By the time we leave, everyone is laughing and making fun of the movie. Tad did a pretty good impersonation of the worse moments.

Tracy calls down the stairs to us, "Are you coming to the beach tomorrow?"

Lucy looks at me before answering. I shake my head slightly; she answers, "No. We have plans."

"Losers!" Tracy closes her door, laughing.

Jeff isn't waiting for us. Lucy looks around for him. "I told him to come later. It's still early. Let's grab a drink. There's a place we're thinking of buying near here."

We walk hand in hand down the street. Lucy puts her other hand on my arm too, hugging me to her. She smiles up at me. "Thanks for a nice night with my friends…even if Josh was an idiot for a little while." I kiss her forehead.

The bar is around the corner. It's full; the side open-air area is packed too. "Good crowd."

"We're not going to get in there." Lucy is dubious, looking at the line of people.

"Have a little faith…" I fake frown at her and tweak her nose. She laughs. "I'll be right back." After talking to the bouncer, I wave Lucy over and we walk right in.

She's still laughing. "How do you do that?"

"I knew the guy. I told him we're interested in the bar and he knows that would be good for him." She's smiling up at me. In the middle of this crowd of people, she's all mine. "That and my charm, of course." She slaps my stomach lightly. I turn her around and we head to the end of the bar.

I order one drink for us to split, getting the bartender's attention with my height. Lucy starts to remove her sweater. "Keep that on."

She halts with one sleeve pulled down, "Why? It's hot in here." She realizes that she just questioned an order and immediately pulls the sweater back on, looking down.

I reach over with both hands and she jerks her chin up and away from me. I only smile and slowly button up the front of the sweater all the way. *I have been too lenient on her today.*

She's swallowing hard, trying not to look at me. I hand her the drink and she takes a small sip, "Thank you." Her little girl voice is barely audible over the crowd, handing it back to me. She squirms so beautifully under my glare, finally blurting out, "I'm sorry!" I only lift a brow, so she adds, "…Sir," quietly. *She's learning fast.*

8 Her

I put my purse down on the bench just inside his apartment and start down the hallway. The calm depth of his voice stops me, though, "Face the wall." I'm so shocked that for a single second I don't move, then quickly turn back to look at him. He nods towards the wall, his face a dark cloud of anger. He didn't seem angry in the elevator; I can't imagine why he's mad now.

I slowly face his wall. "Hands behind your back, Lucy." I slowly move my arms. He walks over to me, standing so close, my hands can feel him. "Head up, eyes straight ahead." I do as he says, swallowing hard, shaking a little. The calmness of his voice, how he's slowly saying this as if I'm a child, only makes me more nervous…and afraid…and wet.

The last time we were in this hall and he was mad at me, he slapped me. I don't know what he's going to do now.

"Lucy, I've been lenient with you today. But I think that this may have been a mistake on my part." He speaks softly right next to my ear, the anger in his voice clearer. "You've shown too many lapses in care. Too many rules you've forgotten today." I know I'm in trouble now. I want to shake my head, plead with him to not be mad at me. But I can't; I've been holding my breath and I'm starting to feel light, like my legs don't belong to me. I'm afraid to move or speak.

"You're going to stand here and think about every rule that you've broken today, little girl, including any from last night. And when I come back, you're going to tell me each one." My eyes are darting in a panic. *He expects me to tattle on myself?* "And *if* you can recite every rule to my satisfaction, you'll go to bed tonight without a spanking." He walks away. I resist the urge to turn my head and look at him.

I can hear him in the bedroom, moving around. He turns on the TV quietly. I'm in a complete panic now. I need to concentrate, but my brain will only focus on how scared I am.

For one second, I think about grabbing my purse and running out the door. But I know I won't. I had my chance to run. After he slapped me, Max had pushed me towards the door and told me to decide to stay or leave. And he told me the next day that was the only chance he was ever going to give me to make a decision for myself. I no longer had a choice of leaving him.

And I knew he was right. My heart no longer had a choice. I'd given in to him…to his anger…his control…his love. I'd given up the right to make any choices, just as he said. My only choice was to love him…to please him…to obey him. *And I've made a mess of that today.* I want to cry, but I think this would only make him angrier right now. *He expects me to be thinking, not feeling sorry for myself.*

I don't know how long I stand like this. I lift my head up more when I hear the TV turn off. He walks quietly down the hall to me, "Time's up, little girl," and grabs my arm to yank me down the hall; my hands fall apart for a moment, "Keep your hands together, behind your back."

He pulls me into the center of the bedroom. My eyes are drawn to the bed. On it is a brown leather belt. One I've not seen before, not one Max would wear. It's too thick and wide. *Oh, my God! He intends to spank me with that*? I panic more, forgetting about my hands, but not dropping my arms in time. I turn to face Max.

His look is still angry, but not as dark. He sits on the edge of the bed, next to the belt. I pivot to follow him. "Undress." I hesitate, but react when he frowns more. I take off my sweater and dress quickly, hesitating only briefly before removing my bra and thong as well.

He raises an eyebrow and says sarcastically, "Do I have to tell you again, Lucy?" I blink twice, before realizing that he means my arms. I put them behind my back and he gives me a small smile. I'm very exposed now. Only my hair covering the top of my nipples provides me any comfort. "Begin."

I'm frozen for four full blinks. I start with last night's slip as he called it, this being the first to come to my mind now. My voice shaking, "I had a drink without you ordering it for me, las…"

He interrupts, his voice deadly calm. "*No*. What is the *rule* you broke?"

I swallow and start over, "I'm not to order anything for myself when I'm with you."

He nods, "Good. Continue."

"I'm not to talk back to you." He nods. "I'm to dress how you like, in skirts and dresses only, but not too revealing." He nods again. "Oh...and I'm not to close any doors to you." He smiles slightly at my eagerness, nodding.

"And I'm not to question your orders." I wait for him to nod.

His face has become unreadable. I try to think if there was anything else, but my mind is a blank. I say the only thing I can, "I'm sorry, Max, please..."

"Very good." It's like a pat on the head, I feel almost giddy. He stands up, bringing the belt with him, though. I can't pull my eyes away from it until he's standing right in front of me. "Take this to the closet. Hang it on the back of the door."

I practically run to do this, but hold the belt away from my body, not wanting it to even touch me.

9 Him

When she returns, I'm sitting back on the bed. "If I tell you to recite rules or if I tell you that you are to be spanked, you will go to the closet and retrieve that belt each time. Do you understand me?"

She answers quickly, not wanting to anger me even slightly now, "Yes, Sir."

I finally put my arms around her, pulling her in for a kiss, taking her arms from her back to be around my waist.

I bought the belt after we came back from my parents' place. It's been hanging on the closet door ever since. I know I'll use it eventually. *But not tonight*. She's still too fragile. Her understanding of how I want it to be between us is still too tenuous. I smile at her and she smiles back. *She has no idea that I'm picturing just how beautiful her ass will be with my belt marks on it.*

I pick her up under her arms and toss her onto the bed. She's laughing, an erotic sound, high and sweet. Her arms are out for me to come to her. I don't get on the bed, only grab her ankles and drag her towards me. "Hands behind your head." She obeys quickly.

With my hands still around her ankles, I pull her legs up. She tries to bend them. "No. Keep them straight." She obeys.

I put her calves on my chest, her pussy tilted up towards me, fully exposed. She's smiling up at me. "I'm not a circus act, you know...don't bend into a pretzel..."

I slap her right tit. Not too hard, but enough to send a shock to her face. "You'll do exactly as I tell you, little girl. Won't you?"

"Yes, Sir." I can hear the lust in her voice, the pleading that I take her right now. I smile at her again. Her face doesn't change, still all longing and apprehension.

I push on her legs and see the muscles stretch and tense. I pinch her nipple and her look gets more longing. I move my hand down her stomach, put my thumb into her wet pussy, my fingers press down on her clit. Her moan is long and hard, her eyes close slowly. Her mouth opens, lips wet. Lucy is the most beautiful girl I've ever seen.

I take my thumb out and her moan whines. I move my hand down and her eyes pop open. Her legs tense against me more. "Relax, Lucy. You're not going anywhere," I grin. She knows this is true. If she tried to move, I would be very upset. And she doesn't want to upset me.

My thumb plays with her ass opening, while her eyes plead non-stop, head shaking slightly, but she's no longer pushing against me. "*All* of you belongs to me, little girl." She only nods, still frightened. "Say it."

"A...All of me belongs to you, Max."

I put just the tip of my thumb inside her ass. Her eyes squeeze shut. *So tight.* I push a little further into her. Her eyes remain closed, a low moan, more of a plea escapes her lips. Her head shakes more. But her ass and legs stay still. Pulling my thumb out, I grab both her ankles again and brace her legs against me hard. Her eyes pop open. The look of fear is amplified. I wait a little longer, not wanting to let the look go, before thrusting into her pussy hard.

She screams out. With her legs up this way, I have complete control of how deep I can get into her. I'm lifting her off the bed slightly by her legs, pinning her against me. I wait. She knows what I want. Finally, she squeezes me and I pull out slowly, push in slowly. Her moans stretch and her head tilts back into her hands. I continue just as slow, my own head back, moaning with how deep I can get, her pussy trying to push back, but taking all of me, forced to take all of me.

Leaning into her legs more, pushing into her harder, I keep her on the bed's edge. I thrust hard, several more times, lost in how smooth her legs are against my chest, how wet her pussy is for me, how her moans match mine. I come when I feel the last of her spasms against my cock.

She opens her eyes and smiles at me. Slowly lowering her legs, I help her stand up. "My legs are rubber now." She's laughing though.

"You'll have to start jogging with me. I'll get you in prime shape." I slap her ass. "Start us a bath." Lucy immediately walks off to the bathroom. "...There's salt in a jar somewhere in there," I call after her.

10 Her

We're stuck in traffic, a delivery truck ahead jamming up the streets. *I'm going to be late to work.*

"Keep your phone on you. When I call, I expect you to answer. When I text, I expect an immediate reply. Understood?" I nod slightly at Max, squinting my eyes. I'm trying to think how this will work at work. I have a busy day scheduled with interviews, staff meetings, and now, a new program from Cruela, cross training with the accounting recruitment team. *I'm just not going to be able to answer my phone.*

Max spanks the side of my thigh with a stinging slap. I cry out and look at Jeff in the rearview mirror, who is just turning his eyes quickly back towards the street. I try to put my hand over the spot, but Max grabs it, twisting my wrist. "You're very close to not being able to get out of this car, Lucy." He twists harder before letting go.

I don't try to rub my wrist or thigh again. It's one of his rules. I will have to recite these tonight for him, naked, with the belt waiting next to him. "I'm sorry. I meant, yes, Sir." I know the higher and softer I make my voice the happier he is with me.

It doesn't work this time. "Is the new rule too difficult for you to manage?"

I'm in dangerous water here. "No, Sir...I just...I...I...will...be at work...and..." I can't finish. His face goes so dark, that I'm sure he's going to slap me. I try to melt away from him, without moving. He only stares at me for a long time. His look doesn't change.

"I'm not an unreasonable man, Lucy." Max takes a deep breath, finally softening his face. "I expect you to be able to text immediately. Can you do that?"

"Yes, Sir!" I'm quick to agree to this even though I'm not sure if it's true.

"And *if* you are unable to answer my call, due to your *busy* job," he says this sarcastically, "then I expect an immediate text in response to my call. With the *exact* time that you will be calling me back. Is that clear?"

I again answer quickly, unsure of how I will make any of that work, "Yes, Sir."

When Jeff holds the door for me, I can't make eye contact with him. I only mumble, "Thank you," and rush by him into my building.

On my floor, I head into the bathroom before anyone can see me and duck into a stall. I'm feeling a little calmer since I came up with a plan in the elevator. With my hands shaking a little, I make a text template for Max, so I can quickly send this if I can't pick up one of his calls. 'I'm sorry, Max! I will call you back in minutes. Love L.' I can fill in the minutes based on however long it will be before I can get away with calling him. I make a few more templates in the hopes that they might work generally for responding quickly to his texts.

I take a deep breath and put my phone away, but quickly grab it again. *Shit. Where am I going to keep this on me today?* I can't just leave it on display. Cruela has her own rules. I'll deal with that problem when I get to my desk.

Before leaving the stall, I look at my leg. Max left a perfect pink handprint, fading already. I still can't get over my twin reactions...ashamed and wet.

I left a plain black jacket in the office a while ago. *It goes okay with the black skirt and multi-colored shirt I'm wearing.* And although it's heavy, I can keep my phone hidden and easily available in the pocket. *I'll just be sweating all day. I'll have to bring something lighter for tomorrow.*

I'm just firing up my computer when I get his first text. "I didn't tell you how beautiful you are today." We carry on a two-minute text chat while I start working. I'm smiling through my morning, proud of myself. I text fast, even using just my thumb, so I'm able to pull it off, even in interviews.

He calls just as we're heading into the elevator for lunch. I answer right away. He sounds very pleased with me now.

11 Him

"Did you have a nice time?" Lucy is still dancing, calling it a waltz, but I'm pretty sure it's just a lot of swaying and twirling. Her gauzy, light blue dress touches the ground as she circles around.

"Yes…Yes, I did." She dances over to me again and I capture her in my arms. We kiss and it's very romantic like in the movies, under the stars, a fountain close by, no one else around.

She's laughing into my mouth. "We are going to make a very corny old couple." I smile hearing her talk about our future together.

We're walking through the park, towards where Jeff is waiting for us on the street. Symphony music can still be heard behind us, but just barely. The lights from the tents make the night around us seem darker. LPE sponsors this event every year, a symphony promo for next season, along with a highlight of local chefs.

We're almost to the street, when a hooded man jumps out of a shadow. Lucy gasps and almost falls over her own feet, my arm keeps her standing. The man is armed. "Give me your wallet…and jewelry. Hurry up!"

I move to stand in front of Lucy, blocking his view of her entirely. "Give me your watch, baby." Lucy is hyperventilating behind me, trying to get her watch off. "Calm down, baby." Keeping my eye on the guy, I say this in a controlled, deep voice to Lucy, the one she always responds to, "Give me your watch." I can hear her breath catch, but she hands it to me with both hands shaking. I keep myself squarely in front of her.

I take mine off, too, and take out my wallet, slowly, one-handed. "Here." I hold it out to him.

I see Jeff running towards us. The guy hears his footfalls on the pavement and moves his gun away from us for a second to look over his shoulder. I move a step towards him, but he turns quickly and grabs the wallet and watches out of my hand before running the other way, into darkness.

I'm holding Lucy against my chest by the time Jeff gets to us, a gun in his hand. It's not legal, but it's one of the reasons he's been my driver for the past four years. He used to be a beat cop until a misfire from a young gang member sent him into early retirement. "You all right?" He's aiming his gun towards the direction the guy ran.

"We're all right. Let's get out of here." We both know there isn't much point in a police report; a random robbery in the park wouldn't count for much.

Lucy is crying and shaking. I pick her up and carry her to the car. She clutches herself to me.

She is tucked into herself, knees up on the sofa, long t-shirt pulled over them, arms wrapped around herself. *It's an improvement.* Lucy has been on her side, crying for the last half hour. I make her take a glass from me. She only stares at it. "Drink it, baby."

She takes a small sip, then a bigger gulp, holding it in her mouth with her eyes closed before swallowing slowly. She lowers her head onto her knees and laughs once, her throat sounding raw from tears, "I thought you said bourbon wasn't a girl's drink."

I smile. She's been wrapped up in her own arms or mine for the past hour. *She's coming out of it finally if she can make a joke.* "It's not, but this is a special circumstance...it's just what the doctor ordered to calm you." I rub her hair and take a big drink of my own glass. I'm not shaken like Lucy, I'm pissed off.

With her head still down, her voice muffled by the shirt and knee, "You protected me." She starts to shake more.

I can't have her losing it again. Her hiccupping and crying only just calmed down. Using a voice I know she'll respond to, "Take another drink, Lucy." She looks up instantly. Even in her fear in the park, she listened to me. She takes another sip. "Good girl."

I take the glass from her, sit next to her, and pull her into my arms. She crawls in with the shirt still covering her knees.

"I'll always protect you, baby." I rock her and rub her hair more, "I'll always take care of you." She's calm again.

She looks up at me. "Thank you…I didn't say thank you for…" her eyes tear up, but she doesn't stop, "for protecting me like that."

I smile at her, "That's my job." I kiss her forehead. She actually stretches her legs out, putting her head back in my arms more. "And I love my job." I get a smile out of her for this.

"And what's my job…to cower behind you?" She looks down at her fingers.

"No. Your job is to listen to me." I know that she's not thinking beyond the robbery tonight. *But I am.* "To do nothing else but think about what makes me happy."

She looks into my eyes. She gets that I'm talking about more than tonight. I'm not sure she's steady enough for this conversation, but I'd planned to say these things to her tonight, about her role going forward.

"I want to explain something to you. Are you up to talking?" She nods her head, her chin down. I give her a look that has her replying correctly though. *Good, she is thinking more clearly again.*

"Lucy, do you remember when you and I talked about your work, what you do, for what company, all that?" She gives me a blank stare, blinking. "We haven't, right?" She nods. "And that's because I don't care about what you do right now for a job."

Her face runs through her emotions…blank stare, frown, anger, frown, blank stare. Her expressiveness is just one of the things I love about her. "You don't *care* about what I do?"

I smile and rub her hair more, "I care very much about what you *do*, every minute of every day." She half smiles, but the frown is still in place. "I just don't care about the specifics of your job."

She starts to nod, but only frowns more, "Why not? I mean…if you care so much about me, why don't you care to hear about my day, what stresses I'm under at work, my successes?" *She's heading in the wrong direction.*

"Watch your tone, little girl." She melts more into my chest and gives a small apology. "I don't care about any of that, because I no longer want *you* to care about any of that." I wait for this to run through her expressions until she stops at the blank stare again. "Your job…your *real* job…is to take care of me, us. It's exactly what I already said. To worry only about what will make me happy."

She swallows hard. Her expression says that she has something she wants to say or ask, but is afraid to anger me. I smile. *She has come so far in such a short time.* "Go on…you can speak freely right now." She starts to open her mouth. "Just watch your tone."

She nods once with a small frown. "I…I'm not sure if I understand what you want. I can't…I mean…my job takes up a lot of my time, my effort. I have to…to give a lot of effort towards being good at it right now…to get the next better job, if my boss doesn't step in my way." I let her continue; get it out of her system really. Her fidgeting increases. "I can't…I don't know if I can stop caring about that…"

"I know what you think…like most girls do…that you have to work hard at a career, get ahead, be just as ambitious as a man." She raises an eyebrow to this, but stays quiet. "I don't want a girl who wants to be a man's equal. I want a girl who understands her place." Both eyebrows go up. I wait for her to respond.

It's only a question though, "And what is that…her place?"

"*Your* place," I look down her body, "is right here, exactly where you belong. In my home." Blank blinking stare. "You only have one boss…me. And the next better job is being my wife."

She swallows hard, blinking a lot. "Are you proposing to me?"

I laugh slightly, "No. Not yet anyway." She relaxes a little. "This would *not* be how I would propose, Lucy."

She laughs too, "Good. 'Cause this would suck as a story to have to tell my mom!"

"I want you to understand though what I expect going forward." Her back tightens against me, her face more anxious. "I expect you to put me before anything else, anyone else. This includes your job, your friends, even your family." She takes this in and remains still. "If there's a choice between making me happy and doing anything else, I expect you to choose me."

"I…I'll try…"

"No. That's not a good enough answer, Lucy." She shrinks more away from my anger. Taking a deep breath, I try a different angle to help her understand, "I am giving you *permission* to continue working…for now. But that won't be forever." Her shocked look takes longer to melt into a frown. I know she's still struggling to come to terms with what she knows to be true. Her life falls into two categories now, what I permit and what I don't. I know that my being blunt about it helps her to accept it faster.

I wait until her expression is steady before continuing, "So you no longer need to care as much about your job. You need to care more about your *real* job."

With her expression still frowning, skeptical, "What if…what if by not caring about my job, though…I lose it?"

I smile. She's finally coming around to an understanding. "I already told you. I will always take care of you. You belong to me, Lucy. You *are* mine. And I want you dependent on me."

Another shocked look, lasting only for a few blinks though. "O…K…"

"I'm going to need more than that, Lucy. I need you to acknowledge that we have a new understanding going forward." I keep my voice deep; speaking to her slowly, as a child. S*he always responds best to this.*

"…Yes, Sir…" She is still hesitant, but answers in a clear voice.

"Good girl." I kiss her and the urgency of her kiss back is enough for me to want to stop talking. "Get ready for bed." She knows this means undressing and waiting by the bed with the belt to recite for me. She was actually a very good girl today, but I know she had a few minor slips.

12 Her

"I can't believe you were robbed." Kevin puts his arm around me and gives me one of his bear hugs, pulling me off one foot. "But, *damn*, your boyfriend is my knight in shining." He has a cheesy grin now.

"Hey…Stop imagining Max as *your* boyfriend, perv!" But I'm laughing. I'm still shocked about what happened, but it feels better to laugh about it in the light of day at least.

Laura squeezes my arm more gently, "Do you think the guy would've shot you?"

The three of us are in line for coffee. I'd already told them every detail. "I don't really know. It all happened too fast. Max reacted so quickly and I just froze."

Laura hugs me with one arm too, but gently, "I'm just glad you're okay."

"Yeah…but you lost that gorgeous watch." Kevin is shaking his head. "There's a special place in hell for thieves, ya know!"

"I am sad about losing the watch Max gave me, but I can't feel too bad about it. Max could've been hurt. We both could've," I just shrug. My old watch looks shabby to me in comparison to the Cartier one, but it's still ticking at least.

My phone rings on the way up the elevator. I answer, even though reception is sketchy in the elevator banks. Max has been non-stop calling and texting me so far this morning. I've been able to balance everything, but it's not just the second Grande of the day making me jittery. *He's testing our conversation last night.* He's forcing my acknowledgement that things are different.

"Hi, Lucy. It's Julia. Jake's girlfriend." I freeze. I forgot that I gave her my number the other night. I feel strange talking to her.

"Oh…Yeah. Hi, Julia. How are you?"

"Great, thanks. I have an interview scheduled tomorrow about my promotion. Short notice, right? I'm so excited!"

The phone broke up through that, but I understood what she said. Her excitement was obvious. "Congratulations." I know what's coming next and feel strange again. The elevator doors open and I wave absently to Laura as Kevin and I get off on our floor.

"So…Are you still up for getting together to give me some interviewing tips?"

I say yes. I know that I'll have to clear this with Max, but I can always cancel if he says no. I've done this already with a few happy hours with Tracy and Laura.

"I can't make lunch, unfortunately. But how bout after work, on me? I can meet around your building today if that works for you?" My stomach is in a knot. I say yes again and we pick a place around the corner to meet at 6:00.

"Thanks, again, for doing this, Lucy. Jake really spoke highly about you and I think this is just the edge I'll need to nail the promotion." She hangs up quickly. The knot has taken over my whole body.

I have one more interview to get through before lunch. I made plans with Laura and Tracy to try a new place. Thinking about this, I run to the bathroom and almost throw up my coffee. I'm going to have to call Max soon to talk to him. I decide to wait till after lunch. *I need more food and less coffee in my stomach before that call.*

"Max. It's me. Can you please call me back ASAP? I have something to ask you." I was hoping to get him on the phone. I don't think I should text him. *This is something he'd want me to talk to him about.*

All through lunch, Laura shared the details of the robbery with Tracy. I only added a little. Tracy was just as shocked, but she was angrier in her reaction. "You didn't call the police? Why the fuck not?"

"Max said it wouldn't matter; we'd spend all this time giving a report and nothing would show up anyway."

"Yeah…But then they'd be on the lookout for a guy in the park with a gun, Luce!"

"Jeff is a retired cop…He agreed with Max." I didn't want to argue with her.

"So what, just because Max says no…? You *can* think for yourself, ya know." Tracy had been pushing her dislike of Max more ever since her movie night. She's still with Josh and I think she needs to justify to herself that Max was the problem that night. Besides, I blew off our Wednesday dinner to go to the event with him last night.

"Max protected me. You weren't there. You don't have the right to criticize him or me in this, Tracy." She's not used to me standing up to her. Laura's eyes were saucers.

I left the deli early, taking my order to go. I couldn't deal with arguing with her, fearing asking Max, and dealing with this weird feeling about meeting Julia all at the same time.

On the walk back, I stopped at a bench. The warm sunshine felt good. People watching distracted me. Several men in suits smiled at me, but I ignored them. Since I've been dressing more like Max prefers, I have noticed that the type of guy who notices me is different, slightly older, more conservative, and politer.

I used to get whistles, stares, and even comments sometimes. I never dressed slutty. But since I've followed the rule of dressing more conservative, more feminine, I've been treated with more respect too. *Just one of the ways that Max has changed me…for the better.*

My phone vibrates, only a text. "In meeting. What's up, baby?"

I hesitate asking this way. I know that time is running out though. *If I wait too long, he'll definitely be mad.* But I can't help feeling strange about the whole thing. *It must be from the talk I had with Jake. I wonder how much Julia knows...*

I decide to just ask. If Max says no, I may even be relieved. "I have to ask you about plans tonight."

"Go on."

"Can I meet Julia after work to help her with her interview?"

I wait a long time without a response. I don't take my eyes off of my phone. I have to return to the office, though, so I get up and start back.

He calls just as I reach my building. As I answer, I walk around to the shady side, away from people. He doesn't say hello. "Have you already said yes to meeting Julia?"

I can feel my heart pounding. I want to lie to him, but I know that he'll know if I do. "...Yes. But I was going to cancel if you said..."

He interrupts me, sounding angry and sad at the same time, "What is the *rule*, Lucy?"

I feel as naked and exposed as I do when he says this in the bedroom. Tears are in my eyes, "I'm not to make any plans without talking to you."

"Wrong." He says this quietly, slowly, but it screams in my head.

I panic. "I…I'm…" I can't breathe.

"You are *not* to make plans without getting my permission *first*."

"I'm sorry…Max…I'm sorry." I can feel the tears on my cheeks. I'm huddled against the building like it's February.

"You may meet Julia. You will not drink anything except water. You will not eat anything. You will be at my place before 7:30." He says this quickly, in an angry monotone.

"Oh…Okay…Thank you…" I feel like the air just warmed around me. My face is hot. My silk dress feels heavier. "Sir."

"And Lucy…When you get home, you will go straight to the closet and bring me the belt."

"Yes, Sir." It's a tiny breath. I feel too faint to waste more than that. I hold myself up against the wall.

"Text me the address. Jeff will be waiting for you." He hangs up.

I get my breathing under control, taking big gulps of air. I wipe my tears away quickly too, jabbing at my cheeks with my palms. *I can't believe I've messed up like this!* I've been playing with this fire all along, hoping that he wouldn't catch on that I make plans first and ask him second. I knew the rule; I just hoped that he'd be tolerant in its interpretation.

I have to steady myself a little longer before trying to walk. *He's not going to be tolerant.* I shake all over, but stop myself from crying again.

I numbly walk back inside. In the elevator, I realize that I didn't text him. I send him the address quickly. *Don't want to add to his anger.*

Waiting for Julia, I look at my phone again. Max didn't text or call all afternoon. I don't know which is worse, anticipating my punishment later or missing his presence in my day. I've been quiet and sick all afternoon.

Tracy stopped by around 3:00 and apologized. Said she was wrong to make it sound like I did something wrong; I was the victim of a crime and she didn't want to make it worse on me. I almost cried again. She just thought I was emotional because it was the first time we'd fought about anything. I didn't correct her. But I did tell her my plans later, so I couldn't go to happy hour with her and Laura.

I look at my watch. It's 6:10. *Where is this girl?* I have to leave by 7:10 in order to make sure I'm not late for Max.

I realize in my anxiety of waiting for Julia, that this is a funny twist of irony. *I'm usually the one who is late.* This was one of the first rules Max introduced me to. I've been able to be on time for him. I'm still late in other things; but for Max, I'm always right on time or early. I know this makes him proud.

And I can really see how annoying it is to be late, to make someone wait for you! I also know why this feels weird. There's a secret between Jake and me and Max. Max said on the phone to Jake that he wasn't honest with Julia, about their past, how they grew up. *I certainly don't want her asking me any questions. It's not my place to answer them.*

Julie finally comes through the door, "Hey. Sorry I'm a little late…work work work!" She sits down at the corner booth I picked for us. A waiter comes over and asks for our orders.

"I'm sticking with water, thank you." I answer quickly, taking a sip of the glass in front of me.

"You sure…it's on me?" Julia is smiling, leaning into the table.

"I'm fine. Not been feeling too great since lunch." *Boy is that an understatement.*

"Oh…I'm sorry…we can do this another time…?"

"No." *I imagine Max would never agree again.* "I'm just not going to eat or drink anything." I look at the waiter as I say this. Julia orders a beer.

"So, thank you again for doing this. It means so much to me." Julia is taking out a small notepad and pen.

"No problem. I hope I can be of some help…"

She tells me about the job. It's a regional marketing manager position. "So if I get it, stay a few years, I might be able to get to a national level, then who knows…the youngest VP?" She takes a big drink. "Most likely, I'll have to jump ship to make a move that big, but one step at a time, right?"

"So let's start with the basics. Why do you want the job? Wait…before you answer that… In general, think of your answers from the company's perspective, from what they're looking for in a regional manager. Always bring it back to how you fit not only the written down job description, but the underlying corporate culture. It's your ace. You already know what they want, better than any outside candidate. Okay…go…"

She smiles. "You are good…Okay…" She shakes her head a little, getting into candidate character. She tells me about her current successes and wanting to expand her understanding up the food chain, to really see hands-on all the regional offices in action. She tells me as a side bar that the company rarely hires married women as regional anything. An old school throwback about too much travel for a family-woman. She's going to use her single status and love of local travel to hit home that this is not a problem for her.

"So…You'll have to travel more with this job?"

"A *lot* more. The first eight weeks will be on the road."

"And Jake's okay with that?" I blurt this out.

She looks surprised. "Well…He doesn't have much choice. I want to move up and this is my ticket. He understands that. It's why we haven't gotten married. Well, it's one of the reasons anyway…" She takes another drink. I sip my water, watching her.

I can see what Jake likes about her. Julia is very pretty, a big personality, funny, smart, nice. But I wonder at her ambition. Max clearly doesn't believe women should be this ambitious in business. *Could Jake really be that different, coming from the same family?*

"So what's next?" She's finished writing my last tip down.

I continue giving her advice until my phone buzzes. I gave myself an alarm, so I wouldn't have to keep looking at my watch or phone to know when I need to leave.

Standing outside, I see Jeff waiting with the door open for me. Julia hugs me and thanks me again. "I'll keep my fingers crossed for you."

"Thanks. I should know by the end of the day tomorrow if I'm moving forward to the next interview. It's a panel of the VP of Regional Sales and others. So I may need to pick your brain for that one too."

"You'll do great." We hug again and I hurry to the car.

I'm actually leaving a little early and feel happy for a second, until I remember what's waiting for me. Jeff keeps looking in the rearview mirror at me. I'm sure my beet red face has him worried. "You okay, Lucy? Need some water...I got some up here."

"No. Thanks, Jeff. Just don't want to be late tonight...Max is expecting me before 7:30..." I look at my phone again. Plenty of time, but it would probably be better if Jeff could get me there even earlier. *Although I'd like to delay my arrival as long as I can...*

Jeff smiles at me. It's a strange smile though. Takes me out of my own head for a moment. "Max is a good guy." He continues since I only give him a questioning look back.

"After I was forced to retire…even after I was healthy again…I was one pissed off asshole for a while…"

I don't say anything. Just keep looking at his eyes as they flick back up to me periodically in the rearview mirror. He starts talking again at the next light. "It wasn't until I met Max that I…I saw how a man has to be in control more…of his own anger…himself…*and* the ones he loves."

I am crimson hot now. I know what he's saying to me. *He knows just exactly how things are with Max and me.* I look away and don't look back. When he holds the door for me, I still can't make eye contact. I just rush past him and head straight to the elevator. Max gave me my own key card a while ago.

On the way up, I have to take several deep breaths to still myself. *Maybe this won't be so bad. Maybe his anger is died down by now and he'll only make me recite the rule again, but right this time. Maybe I'm completely kidding myself!*

I'm ten minutes early, but the front door is open. I stop before walking in, listening for Max. "Come in, Lucy." His voice sounds normal. He didn't yell. I can tell he's in the living room, but I can't see him. I can't see if his face is stern or not.

I quietly close the door. Setting my purse down on the bench, I quickly slip my shoes under it. Barefoot, I walk down the hall, one foot in front of the other, almost on tiptoe.

Turning the corner, I see Max is sitting on the sofa. He's only wearing sweatpants. The TV is on, but muted. The room is bright. I stop to stare at him, but he doesn't look up at me. "You're early. That's good." His voice is still steady, deep, but not angry. *Maybe I have lucked out!*

"Don't you have something to do?" He still hasn't looked at me. I blush all over. I pivot around and walk on tip-toe towards the bedroom. I've made this walk many nights before, to get the belt and bring it to him, in the bedroom, the living room, the den, even on the terrace. But never *knowing* that he will use it on me. Always with a hope that he won't. The closet seems very far tonight. The belt is extra heavy.

I'm shaking when I lay it on the sofa next to him. He still doesn't look at me. I know what comes next. I undress in front of him and put my hands behind my back. My eyes are dry from staring at him for so long, not blinking. My lips are dry from breathing quick, shallow breaths, all my spit gone, my throat scratchy and working overtime swallowing. I can do nothing but stand, waiting for him.

And he takes his time. He's not even looking at me. I forget about all my discomforts, how my arms feel numb from squeezing them behind my back, my stomach muscles hurt from holding them in the way he taught me. I can only think...*please, look at me...*

13 Him

I went for a run when I got home. I had to do something to work off this steam. I didn't call or text her this afternoon. My anger was too fresh. And I wanted to give her time to really think about what she did. *And what she has coming.*

The run helped. I'm more level-headed again. Waiting for Lucy to arrive, I even smile. *I've waited for this night for some time.*

I knew that starting with a spanking wasn't the right way with her. Lucy would have been overwhelmed with all the demands of a regimented punishment like this. She would have been unable to follow all my instructions at one time. And a spanking is a very special form of punishment. I needed her head to be in the right place for this.

Slapping her was enough the first time. She understood that her body was no longer hers. *She's mine and I'll do as I please with her.*

I've trained her in how to take a more rigid, more strenuous, punishment. She's come so far in her level of submission, her eagerness to please me. She knows what I expect of her now.

And I look forward to giving her a first spanking.

I stand up, making Lucy take a step back, eyes wide. I take the belt with me. Her eyes follow my every movement, the fear pulsing off of her.

"Follow." I can hear her bare feet behind me as I walk into the bedroom, not turning around.

I stop next to the closet. "Face the wall." She immediately does.

I stand behind her. "Head up." She obeys, jolting her chin high. "Put your hands on the wall, flat." She does. "A little farther apart...shoulder length." *She's going to need the support,* I smile to myself. "Now bring your legs back two steps, bottom up." From this angle, her back is arched, muscles tensing in her arms. *She's beautiful.* Her bottom is offered to me. "Good girl. This is how you will stand when you receive a spanking with the belt against the wall."

She whimpers a quiet, "Yes, Sir." I know the humiliation of standing this way, waiting for her punishment, is torturing her. And I like making her wait.

"You won't move from this position. If you move, I will start your punishment over. Do you understand me?"

"Yes, Sir." It's a little stronger this time, a pleading to get started, to finish.

I rub my hand down her back, her whole body convulses. This being her first spanking, I want to see how she reacts, how her body responds before starting.

With my left hand, I smack only one cheek, towards the bottom. Not too hard. She cries out though, more from shock. I smile and smack the other cheek, higher up, less of a cry, less shocked. The slight pinkness fades quickly. *Good.* I don't want to bruise her. *Not on this first spanking.*

A spanking is special, controlled; I can keep my own anger in check, following a simple pattern. I can hurt her, but I won't get carried away. *Just far enough.* There may be times when she is unable to leave the bed after a spanking, legs and ass too swollen or sore. But not tonight, not the first time. *She just may not be able to sit for a few days, but that's up to how well she does.* I smile.

I step back and she gasps and tenses. She's anticipating too much. "Close your eyes, Lucy. And remember to breathe." She can only nod her head, but I can see that she obeyed.

I snap the belt in my hands, she flinches, but her eyes stay closed. *Good.* I don't want her tensing up too much.

The first spank of the belt lands dead center of both cheeks. A perfect pink patch flares. She gasps her cry out, leaning on the wall, head lowered slightly. "Head, up, Lucy. Or I start over." She immediately obeys. "If you move at the wrong moment, I could hurt you...unintentionally. You need to remain still for this. Do you understand me?"

"...Yes, Sir...I'm sorry, Sir!" *Such a good girl.*

I strike the same spot, bringing a deeper pinkness and gasped cry back. I wait for her breathing to even again, she stays in position this time. The third and fourth are quick, above and below slightly the last two, a little harder. Her cry is gulped down and escapes as a high pitched hiss. Her bottom is a beautiful cherry.

"How many times did you break the rule, Lucy?"

I wait patiently behind her. Her mind is dueling between animal pain and her desire to please me. I wait for her desire to reach the surface. "Five, Sir...I'm so sorry...please...I'm sorry...ple..."

"No. No begging!" She stops, her body shaking. "How many times have I spanked you already?" I know the answer, but I want to force her to say.

"Four, Sir." A more pathetic sound of pleading could not be heard; I smile.

"You have one more coming then." She tenses every muscle in her back, legs, arms. Her hands grip the wall. *My sweet girl.* "Calm down. Breathe, baby." I wait for her to relax a little. When she is just starting to calm, I let the belt crack hard across her lower bottom, the sweet sitting spot, the one I know will hurt the most. She strangles a cry, a yelp of pain, her legs dancing and shaking for a moment. But she stays in position.

"Hands behind your back." She is only too happy to comply if this means the punishment is over.

"Apologize, *not* beg, Lucy." I stand right behind her, the belt still in my hand.

"I'm sorry, Sir." She's strong, no hesitancy.

"And thank me for punishing you."

She swallows. "Thank you, Sir."

I put my hand in her hair, give a slight tug, but mostly rub her softness. She's so small, so soft, so yielding. "I like hurting you, Lucy." She rubs her head against my hand, the obedient puppy. "I like that you give yourself to me completely. That I can cause you pain and fear. I can make you my good girl again with my belt or my hand..." I lower my hand to her ass. It's still a little warm, the pinkness not quite faded. I pinch her lower cheek, not hard, but it's tender enough to squeeze the breath out of her. "That's what punishment does. It makes you my good girl again. You want that, don't you?"

"Yes, Sir." Her whole body answers, trying to sway closer to me, but not moving from her spot, arms still held tight against her back.

"And you will always be my good girl. I will always *make* you my good girl, Lucy. I love you."

14 Her

The pain is only a small part. The initial shock of being hit with his belt is only a part of it. The humiliation of standing, waiting, for this...*that's the hardest part*. Knowing that I'm waiting for Max to hurt me. That I stand here, as a grown woman, waiting for a spanking from my boyfriend. *No...*

...That I stand here deserving a spanking. That's the humiliation. That I've done this to myself, gotten myself into this. If I'd only just behaved, followed his rule.

The smacks seem to hit all over; my ass is a giant bullseye and Max has deadly aim. I'm screaming in my mind, but only tiny cries escape.

Thinking of the number of times these past weeks that I've done this, made plans, then asked permission, my face burns with heat. I want to beg for his forgiveness, make him understand that I won't ever do that again. *I'll be good!* I won't disappoint him again. I won't make him angry again.

The last one...*the pain*...I forgot about thinking, breathing, anything, until my lungs hurt and I take a shattered breath in and out.

"I'm sorry, Sir." I know this is a part of the ritual; the routine of punishment that I've become familiar with.

"Thank you, Sir." *This is new*. I want to plead, beg still. All I can do is thank him for spanking me and wait, hopeful that this is enough, that I'm deserving of his love still. *Please*!

"...I will always make you my good girl, Lucy. I love you." And I begin to shake. These words smack the bullseye in my brain. I need his love. I need his discipline. I need him.

"Turn around." I spin quickly, eyes hungry to see his face.

Max kisses my forehead and wipes my cheeks. I wasn't aware that tears had fallen, that my shame bubbled up and slipped from my eyes. He tilts my chin up and kisses me fully, the warmth of his mouth spreading down my stomach, into my pussy.

I'm wet. I only just realize how wet. It's from the spanking, from the humiliation. I swallow. I don't recognize myself, a hungry pet waiting for a bone. I almost laugh, a little dizzy. I swallow this back, a squeak instead.

"You may put the belt away." I quickly take it from him and open the closet door. The belt hangs as a constant reminder. I come back to stand in front of him, my arms back in place.

Max smiles at me, watching me. "Follow." He walks to the bed and removes his pants. I am panting...*stop panting*...staring at his hard ass and legs. I want to bite his shoulder; I want to taste him.

He lays back on the bed, head propped on a pillow against the headboard. "Keep your arms back and get on me."

I'm not graceful, I almost fall face first onto his lap, my knees sinking in the softness of the bed, but he keeps me up with his hands on my shoulders, smiling at me. I position myself over his cock. I can feel my wet lips pressed against him. My knees squeeze his hips.

Putting his hands on my waist, Max lifts me onto his erect cock. In a quick thrust, pushing me down by my hips, he enters me. Full length. Full force. I gasp in pain and deepened desire fulfilled. His hand on my stomach keeps me up. "Ride me."

My eyes pop open. Technically, I've never done this before. I tried once, at a drunken night out in a back seat with my last boyfriend.

I awkwardly try lifting myself, feeling my thighs squeezing, my sore ass tightening. "Use your hips, rock back and forth more with them." My arms behind my back make this more difficult. I squeeze my hands against my elbows to steady myself and try again, using my hips more as Max instructed. I can feel his length sliding inside me. The depth and pressure is equally pleasing and painful. I get used to the rhythm, going slow, not taking him all the way in or all the way out.

He grabs my hips and sits me down hard on his cock. My eyes fly open at the pain. "All the way, Lucy." I only nod my head, trying to get the rhythm with this much up and down, back and forth with my hips. I lean forward slightly, my knees shaking against his sides, my thighs straining, keeping my balance. He finally grabs my waist and with his arms flexed, jackhammers me easily against his cock. I push my hips into him to join his thrusts and he smiles, "Good girl."

After a few minutes like this, "Ask me." His breath is jagged. I know what he wants.

"Please...can I...please...?" my breath panting each word with his thrusts.

"Yes...yes, my good girl." We come together. He continues thrusting, his throbbing inside me making the ache a dull aftershock of pleasure.

I open my eyes again and Max is smiling at me. He reaches up and brushes my hair off my face. "You are the most beautiful girl." I blush. "And you're all mine." I smile shyly back. "You may move your arms, Lucy."

I release my hands, realizing how strained my shoulders were from my grip.

15 Her

"I nailed the interview!" Julia is yelling into my phone. I pull it away from my ear a little. I'm waiting for Max on the street. A few people walk by, looking at me. *She's so loud.*

"That's great. Congrats, Julia."

"Let's celebrate! I want to thank you over some bubbly."

"Oh...that sounds great...I'll need to talk to Max first..." I absently rub my hand over the side of my hip. It's as close as I can get to soothing my sore butt in public. My ass is no longer on fire, but it's still a little swollen and sore on the very bottom. The color is a deep red too. Sitting for interviews was torture today.

"I think Jake is already calling him. I'm on my way to meet him now. Hopefully, we'll see you tonight. Or we'll make plans for later this weekend. Thanks, Lucy, you really helped. Can't wait to tell you all about it."

Julia was so excited, that I didn't even get a word in, other than to say that I'd call her about plans, before we hung up.

I see the car pulling around the corner. I'm excited myself. After last night, I could really use a night just relaxing with Max, being in his arms, just us. I need to be around him. I need to feel his arms around me. This morning I was like a puppy, following him around the apartment as he got ready. I've been obsessed with looking at my phone today, a little disappointed that he didn't call more, but happy that I got a text every hour.

I've been so distracted today with what he did to my butt and how much I want to show him my love by being such a good girl for him. *I can't even believe this is how I'm phrasing it in my own head. ...My, what a spanking will do to a girl!*

But my hopes for a night with Max all to myself crumble when Jeff opens the door for me and I see Dan. He gets out so I can sit in the middle next to Max. Scooching over the seat makes me wince and take a quick breath in. Max only smiles at me, "Jeff has a pillow for you if you'd like."

"What's wrong, Lucy, did you hurt yourself?" Dan is back seated, next to me now.

I turn my eyes to Max as I answer though, "I'm fine." I'm beet red and my ass is throbbing, but I don't want to see the knowing look in Jeff's eyes again. He smirked at me getting into the car this morning. He was extra gentle helping me out with his arm though. *And I definitely don't want to explain anything to Dan.*

Lucky for me, Dan drops it. Max kisses me and I relax a little more. Each bump in the damn city streets isn't a picnic though. It's really only one spot that's still a little sore, but it's right where I sit. *And I've had to sit all day.*

"So I hear you were a big help to Julia…"

I'd actually forgotten about her call in my attempts to keep my ass from feeling the worse of the potholes. "Oh…yeah…she was going to do great on her own. I just provided a few tips to give her more courage." I turn to Max, "Did Jake call you?"

"Yeah," his look darkens only for a second. "We're heading there now to meet them."

This is definitely not going to be the quiet night I wanted. I say a little prayer to any powers that be, *please, don't let me do anything to make Max mad tonight…I don't think my ass could take it.*

Dan holds the door for us and Max subtly rubs my butt as we enter the club. He's gentle but it still stings. And he pats a little harder once before stopping. I have to swallow back my wince this time. He'd already told me that one of the special things about a spanking is that he can continue to administer little reminders to behave so easily like this. His slightest touch is enough to warn me against doing anything wrong tonight.

"Yay! You could make it." Julia jumps up and grabs me in a hug. I'm pulled off balance and she lets go too quickly, so I fall back onto one of the low lounge seats. It's cushy, but my ass would feel like it was nails no matter what I sat on right now, let alone land on hard. I actually squeak and press my eyes and lips together tightly for a second. Julia doesn't notice, she's too busy hugging Dan and Max hello.

But Jake notices. From his seat opposite me, he notices everything. I try to sit more comfortably, keeping his gaze though, afraid to let it go. Jake's eyes narrow, lips tightening, jaw clenching. He's a mirror to Max in his dark looks. I pray that he won't say anything right now. I plead this with my eyes.

Max sits down next to me, putting his arm around me. "Hello, little brother." He of course notices the way Jake keeps staring at me. He didn't see my quick sit-down though, since Julia was bear hugging everyone. He didn't see that Jake saw my pain.

"How are you doing, Lucy?" Jake asks this pointedly, not looking at Max.

"I'm *fine*, Jake." I say this in a strong voice.

Jake doesn't drop his stare. Julia sits back down next to him. He still keeps staring. I finally look away from everyone. I don't want to see the look on Max's face either.

Extra glasses are brought to the table and Julia jumps up to pour champagne in each one.

I look to Max to make sure that it's okay; he kisses my nose and hands me a glass from the table himself. When we all have glasses in hand, Julia stands up again. Jake only glances at her; he keeps his eyes on me still.

"I just wanted to thank you, Lucy, for all your help yesterday. And I want to celebrate with you guys this hopefully next big step for me." We all clink glasses and I'm grateful for the cold bubbles on my throat.

"So…Regional Manager. That *is* a big step, Julia." Max is smiling, but I know that he's mocking Jake more than congratulating Julia. Jake knows it too. "What region will you be managing if you get this promotion?"

"Southeast, coastal. It's a *huge* market for us, very competitive." She has her hand draped over Jake's knee.

Dan interjects, "That's a sweet area to cover. No winters."

"And will you have to travel to the Southeast, coastal area often, Julia?" She is oblivious to the tone in Max's voice. He's provoking Jake.

"Yeah, it's a pretty travel intensive job. Like I told Lucy, the first eight weeks will be on the road. At *least* eight weeks." She takes a big drink and doesn't see the look Jake shoots her. He obviously didn't know this. *She didn't even talk to him about it?* "Then who knows? …Probably two to three weeks out of the month."

"Julia…" Jake starts and she turns to look at him. She stops a little shocked at the look on his face. It's a pained look, an embarrassed look.

She only taps her hand on his knee, "I told you all this, Jake. About how important this job would be for me. And that it involved travelling." She's already turning away from him.

"No, Julia." His voice is so like Max's that it makes me shiver for a second. The anger is clear. Julia is still ignoring it though, not looking at him at all, only topping off her own glass. "You never mentioned that you would be travelling non-stop for eight weeks, then gone for most of every month. I *would've* remembered that."

"Well…" She looks embarrassed, looking around at all of us for a moment, then back to Jake, "Well, sweetie…let's talk about this later. Tonight we're celebrating. I still have to *get* the job anyway."

She stands up. "I gotta pee. Lucy you wanna come with me? The bathroom in this place is great. They have free perfume samples." She walks around the table, and stands behind Jake, waiting for me.

It pains me to see the look on Jake's face. It's a perfect chemistry of anger, hurt, and disappointment. *I'm glad that I've never seen that look on Max's face*. I turn to Max and he nods slightly. I stand up and am relieved for a moment, then my ass starts throbbing again from sitting for too long.

16 Him

"I really wasn't expecting her to say all that, Jake." I lean in towards him, my palms up on my knees. "I'm sorry."

Jake just shakes his head, holding it with his hands, looking down at his lap.

"Maybe she won't get the job…" Dan adds lamely.

"No…No. Julia will get the job. Julia gets everything she goes after." Jake sits back heavily in the chair, his hands still holding the sides of his head, tilting back to stare up at the ceiling. He runs his fingers through his wavy brown hair and pushes a breath out loudly.

"So what are you going to do about it?" I'm still sitting forward. Watching my brother hurt like this is hard, but I'm hopeful that this is the last straw with Julia, that he'll realize that she's not the girl for him.

"*Do* about it?" Jake drops his hands and glares at me, the look of anger back in his eyes. *Good. He needs to get angry about this.* "What *can* I do about it, Max?" He continues to stare at me. I say nothing.

"Well...maybe you could talk to her...ya know...see if maybe there's another promotion that she can go after instead..." Dan is trying to help, but he doesn't understand what's really being said here.

"What would *you* suggest I do, Max?"

"That's up to you, Jake. You know your *options*." I keep my voice low and steady.

"Like what? S*panking* her like you do Lucy?" Jake says this quietly.

Dan just laughs, until he sees the looks we're exchanging. He catches on that Jake is being serious; or that I'm at least taking him seriously.

"Yes. If you think that would help." I answer slowly. I ignore the wide-eyed look from Dan. "You know my opinion...she's never been the right girl for you, Jake."

Jake leans forward now too. "And that is *none* of your business, Max. Why don't you take care of your own shit? Like why Lucy isn't able to sit still tonight."

Dan starts to say something, but I answer Jake first, "Lucy can't sit because she *lied* to me. She broke my rule and she paid the price. If you listened to your own heart, you'd know that that is the way it should be between you and Julia too. But it never will be with her, will it?"

Jake just shakes his head, staring at me. Dan stares in disbelief at us both.

Lucy returns to the table alone, "Julia is on the phone with someone from work I think…she'll be right back." She freezes her smile when she sees the three of us though. She knows something happened while she was gone, just not what. She slowly lowers herself onto her seat. Dan and Jake both watch her, with Dan staring at her ass.

I put my hand on her knee. She reaches for her glass, but I stop her. "No. We're leaving soon." She sits back. Dan just blinks at us, like he's watching his favorite TV show. Jake glares at me.

When Julia does return, he jumps up. "We're leaving."

"What? Where are we going? I just told some work folks to meet us here." Julia sits down. Jake grabs her arm and pulls her to her feet. Julia yanks her arm out of his grip. "You're hurting me! Jake what has gotten into you?" He just looks at her for a long moment with his jaw clenching. No one else moves or says anything. He finally takes a deep breath, but remains standing.

"Julia." He picks up his messenger bag and continues a little softer, "Julia…I wish you all the best. But we both know that this isn't working out." She opens her mouth to say something, still looking around embarrassed at us. "No. I don't want a part-time girlfriend. And you only want a full-time career." He leans over and kisses her shocked cheek, "You'll do great on the new job. I'll sleep at a friend's tonight. We'll sort out the apartment tomorrow." He turns and walks away.

I get up to follow him, but he turns on me with his arms in the air. "Leave me alone, Max. Not now." I watch him walk out the door, finally seeing the brother I knew was in there. *He's finally taking control of his own life again.*

When I return to the table, Lucy is looking beautifully concerned and shocked. I sit down next to her and take her hand, "He'll be all right."

Dan just continues to stare, mostly at Lucy.

Julia is downing a glass of champagne. "I *can't* believe this. I just can't fucking believe *him*." She glares at me, her voice going up in volume. "*You* put him up to this, didn't you? You've never liked me, have you, Max?"

"I like you Julia. Just not for my brother." I say this evenly, quietly. People are starting to stare at our table.

"Let's go." Lucy stands with me; Dan jumps up when he realizes we're leaving.

"Fine…just leave. But you tell Jake that if he wants back in that apartment with me, he'll have to *beg* my forgiveness for tonight!" Julia yells this as we walk away.

On the street, "How bout a cup of coffee?" Dan only nods his head. Lucy looks pleadingly at me. "Yes…we're going for coffee. I think Dan would like to ask you something…" Lucy looks wide-eyed at Dan. He only sheepishly starts walking down the street next to us.

17 Her

"We'll have one decaf, one regular, please." Max is doing the ordering as usual. I know the decaf is for me; he's told me not to drink so much coffee, since I have a hard time sleeping if I have any in the afternoon. It was hard at first, but I'm getting used to it. Dan orders coffee too.

I think we're all a little shaken by what happened with Jake. No one's talking. I'm not surprised, though; I know Max has been working on him for the past year, ever since he moved in with Julia. Max has a strict rule against living together.

I smile at this, though, since we are practically living together. Every night we're at his place now. But I do still have my own apartment, nothing's official yet.

Max puts his hand on my knee and looks at Dan directly. We're in a quiet diner, only a few people around; but Max still sat us in a corner booth off by ourselves.

Dan is just putting his phone down on the table, "Becca will be here in a half hour. She's finishing up some details with the show." He avoids making eye contact with me, only stares at Max, who has the oddest smile on his face. It's like he's laughing, encouraging, and challenging Dan with quirks of his lips.

I don't think I want to know what went on tonight while Julia and I were in the bathroom. I have a sinking feeling.

"So...where do you kids wanna eat tonight?" Dan is trying to lighten the mood, but Max isn't having any of it.

"Why don't you say what's on your mind *really*, Dan. We're all friends here..."

Dan shoots a look at me, but quickly looks down at the table, darting back up to Max. This feels like a tennis match and I'm afraid I'm the ball. *I don't want this to go on.* I reach my hand across the table, not to touch Dan but just reaching towards him. Both men follow my hand and stare as it rests close to Dan's fingertips, still on his phone. "You can say anything you want, Dan. Ask whatever you want..." I say this quietly, unsure of myself. It has the desired effect, though. He finally looks me in the eye with a combination of puzzlement and concern.

Max hasn't moved. He just continues to look at Dan, his face completely calm and unreadable. Except I can see the small movements of emotion. The one that surprises me is hope.

"Is Max hurting you?" Dan chokes this out, so quiet that the words are almost lost in their endings.

"No." I see Max's face move slightly. I know what he expects and I still don't know if I'm ready for it.

"Did he..." Dan shoots a quick look to Max, changes directions and stares now with a little anger towards him, "*Did* you hurt her?"

"Yes." Max remains calm, waiting for his friend to adjust to this answer before continuing. "I spanked Lucy because she misbehaved."

My body is heating up. I look down at my hand, still on the table. The waitress puts the coffees in front of us and we don't reach for them. I just move my hand back onto my lap.

When she's out of hearing, Dan finally speaks. "Are you crazy? Why are you telling me this?"

"Because I'm not going to hide who I am. Certainly not from my *best* friend." Max leans forward a little, intensely staring at him.

Dan only shakes his head, looking down at his hands on the table, palms facing each other, like he just heard something absurd. Max waits for him to say something. Finally, he meets Max's eyes again, "Max...we *are* best friends. I think of you as family." Max nods to this. "But...but I can't *condone* you hurting your girlfriend."

Before Max can answer him, though, I speak up. *I won't have Dan thinking less of Max, not because of me.* "He's not." Both men turn their heads to me, Max smiling slightly.

"He *just* said..." Dan can't say the rest.

"I know what he said. But he's not *hurting* me...," my voice is stronger this time. I look at my hand though, still unsure of what to say next. I reach for my coffee and take a small sip. "I have agreed to follow Max's rules. I broke a rule. And I knew the consequence." I say it quickly, trying to keep my voice from squeaking at the end. With my eyes down, I can still see that Dan is staring in disbelief at me. Max squeezes my knee slightly. I'm sure my face is turning purple from the humiliation now. "Believe me...it *does* hurt," I glance quickly at Max, who grins, "But...but I'm *fine*." I finish this and look directly into Dan's eyes again.

Dan sits back, hands in his lap, watching me. Max also sits back, watching Dan. Their tennis match is back on.

"Well...fine...then, fine..." He shakes his head again, "If this is how you want it...then fine. But why tell *me*?"

Max answers, "Because I needed Jake to see that I'm not ashamed of who I am. Who he is really if he'd admit it to himself."

"Jake does this too?"

Max only smiles, "No...Not with Julia obviously, anyway. But it *is* how we were raised." Dan's look of shock goes supernova. He doesn't even blink for a long moment. Max keeps talking, "Look, Dan...I get that this isn't everyone's idea of how it should be between a couple, but I needed my brother to see that it's okay that it is to us." He takes a drink, a pause to give Dan time to think that through, before continuing, "And I needed to know that Lucy could stand up for this too. She *should* be ashamed for earning a punishment. But I don't want her ashamed for how she is

with me or that I *do* punish her." He squeezes my knee
again.

I hadn't heard him say all this so succinctly before.
Somehow hearing it said out loud to someone else, I feel
more at ease, more confident and safe with Max. I squeeze
his arm and he smiles at me, kisses my nose. Dan is
watching us.

"So you did this for Jake and Lucy...but what about
me? How am I supposed to just go back to how things were,
Max? Pretend I don't know all of this?" Dan is searching
Max's face for answers.

"You knew something was different with Natalie. You
just never wanted to know the truth. I haven't been myself
with a girl in a long time, not since before we met, Dan. I
tried with Nat, but she rejected her own feelings." I'm
swallowing hard hearing this. Max hasn't talked about any
past relationships. He refuses to hear about any of mine.
"You know how upset I was for so long after Nat." Dan nods
to this, even softens his look of skepticism. "I want you, as
my family, my best friend, to be a part of our lives. Mine
and Lucy's. And I knew that meant that sooner or later, you'd
have to know the truth. I said before, I don't want to hide
who I am from you."

Dan takes his time thinking about all this. His look
softens even more. But before he can say anything, Becca
shows up. She sits down and takes a sip of his coffee. "Are
we eating here or elsewhere, kiddos? I'm starving."

"I'm starving too." I try to break the thin layer of ice
hanging over our heads. Dan smiles at me, it's a small smile,
but it's there at least.

"And I'm dying to know what happened tonight with Jake." Becca is leaning in towards Max.

Dan cuts in though, "I'll tell you later." He says this to Max, but again with a smile. "Let's go to the place with the good noodles...down the street..." He and Becca discuss which place he means, arguing over who has the best noodles.

I only snuggle into Max's arm more. He kisses my cheek and says into my ear, "I'm proud of you." It sends that same electric current from my stomach to my pussy. Dan is watching us again.

18 Him

I hang up. Jake still won't answer my calls. I've left him voicemails and texts, but he needs his space. Dan said he hadn't heard from him either.

Dan. I shake my head thinking about him. It's been a week since Jake left Julia, since Lucy confessed to Dan that she's fine with me disciplining her, since he accepted all this. He surprised me at the office on Wednesday. Asked if I would go for a drink with him. I called Lucy and told her to wait at home for me. I haven't let her go out all week. Continued punishment for her lies, she's grounded from seeing her friends outside of work next week too.

Dan was shy about talking, but I just waited him out. Finally, he blurted out that he'd told Becca about Lucy and me. He'd laughed.

"Becca wasn't even surprised or shocked at all." I wasn't surprised by that. She has more understanding of relationships than Dan. He tends to be more of a what you see is what you get kinda guy. It was harder for him to think that there was more to what he suspected all along. He's coming around though.

"She said she always thought you were kinky." Dan said this with a big laugh. Of course, he added that his wife didn't really give my sexual preferences much thought. Not really, of course, with more laughter. "She even said it's in all of her favorite smut books, so who knows..." He'd looked embarrassed, but we cheered to ourselves for finding happiness. He finally accepted that Lucy and I *are* happy with our arrangement.

He also asked if I told Mike. I told him I intend to, when the time is right of course. I don't want any more secrets or hiding. He only nodded at this. He doesn't want to be put in the middle of anything. He knows I wouldn't do that to him, though.

I hear Lucy getting out of the shower. *Good.* I smile to myself thinking of the afternoon she has in store.

"Lucy, come here." I use my deepest voice, barely louder than normal. She is standing in the doorway in an instant, hair dripping down her wet body, towel pressed to her side.

"Can I dry off first?" *She knows better than this.* I clench my jaw, but she jumps to come to me before I have to do more than this.

She tries to put the towel around herself to stop from puddling on the floor. I grab it out of her hand and throw it on the ground. Water runs down her legs, off her hair; drops magnify her erect nipples. Her gorgeous look of fear is perfect. She puts her arms behind her back automatically. *My good girl.*

"Lucy, last week I administered a punishment for what misbehavior?"

"I didn't get your permission before making plans." She says this quickly. *She's not likely to forget that rule any time soon.*

"And have you done this since then?" I already know the answer.

"No, Sir." She looks down, "You grounded me. And I wouldn't ever do that again. Sir." She is quick to add, in case I mistook her words for pouting. *She is a good student.*

"Good." I sit on the bed. "Go get the belt." She stops herself from saying anything, but her whole body twitches with fear and the question I know she's thinking. "Don't make me tell you again, little girl." This has her moving quickly to the closet.

She comes back just as quickly, laying the belt next to me. Her flesh is goosebumps, her nipples painfully erect and darkened; her hair still drips water down her back and tits. Her arms are back where they should be.

"Lucy, you have a spanking coming today." She tears up, but doesn't do more than quiver her lips at this. Such a beautiful look of fear and dismay is on her face. She's shouting her pleas with those blue eyes. She takes a stuttered breath in and holds it, calming herself as I've taught her. "This is a maintenance spanking, Lucy." I give her a moment to react. "If I have to punish you, then the next week you will receive a spanking as a reminder to be good." Her eyes look down for a second; she knows she can't argue with me. My pride mixes with my desire for her. "Even if you've been on your best behavior all week long, as you *should* be anyway...you will receive a spanking. Do you understand me?"

"...Yes, Sir..." She says through swallows. Her bottom is only just back to a normal color. She had trouble sitting for two days afterwards. *I'll be easier on her today...but she doesn't need to know that.*

"Get over my knees." She moves jerkingly, awkwardly placing herself across me, putting her fingertips on the floor. "Place your hands around my calf; this will keep you steady." She does this and moves a little to adjust herself again. "Put your legs straight out. And keep your toes pointed." She does, stretching her body, exposing her creamy white upper thighs to me. I adjust her a little so her bottom is raised higher on my knee. I can feel her heartbeat. I know this position strains her leg and stomach muscles.

"Do not move from this position until I give you permission. If you move your hands or your legs, I will start your punishment over and add additional spankings for disobedience. Do you understand me, Lucy?"

"Yes, Sir." I can tell that she wants to get this over with quickly. *Not gonna happen, little girl.*

I place my hand gently on her ass and feel her flinch. *God, how I love her!* Her hair covers her face, but I know she's blushing; her soft tears will blend with her wet hair nicely. I admire how my hand can cover a cheek completely. I rub down to the fold just above her thighs, her most tender spot. I can feel her wet heat from here, too. "Open your legs." She obeys without hesitation, rocking slightly. She keeps her legs stretched, toes pointed though.

I cup my hand over her pussy, rubbing down to her clit, she moans. "Quiet." *She's going to need another shower*, I smile to myself. "Does waiting for your punishment make you wet, little girl?"

She whimpers, but answers in her sweet, girlie voice, "...Yes...Sir."

"Does getting a spanking make you wet?"

"...Yes, Sir..."

"Why?" I can tell that she's startled by the question. Her mind is already down the path of waiting for pain, an animal place, a pet waiting for its master's pleasure. This makes her crawl back a little from fear, up to a point of being able to think. It takes some deep breaths before she can answer.

"I want to please you."

"That's not your only reason, Lucy." I chastise her.

"When you said...that...that you liked...hurting me..." I wait patiently for her to continue, absently stroking her pussy and clit. "...I wasn't able to tell you...that...I like that you do... That I know it's how you show me how much you love me. Even when I'm bad, you make me your good girl again...and I want to be good for you..." She's crying softly, this raw revelation taking her breath and turning it into sobs. "I crave your love, Max. I need your love. The pain...is part of your love and I crave it." She says this with a strangled voice, tears choked back.

I wait for her to calm a little more. "You do make me so happy, Lucy. I love you. And I *will* always make you my good girl."

I don't wait. I spank her tender spot first, a quick sting with only my hand. She whimpers, but stops herself. I pick up the belt and her legs stiffen. She tries to relax; I don't wait. I smack both cheeks with the belt, dead center. Her breath goes in sharply, but she remains quiet otherwise. The second and third strikes follow each other quickly, both centered. Her breathing is rapid. I wait only a second more and give her one good smack to her cheek bottoms, the belt hitting the very top of her thighs as well. Her breath stops for a second. I bring the belt down one more time on the same spot. A small cry escapes with her breath.

"You may raise your legs, Lucy." She instantly brings up her feet, "That's high enough." She stops with her toes pointed perfectly up to the ceiling. "You may not lower your legs onto your bottom. You'll feel the sting of your punishment without any relief, little girl." I let her breathing even out before having her stand. She puts her arms in position and waits for me to tell her what to do. *Such a good girl, I have.*

Her tears always make me harder. Her face is soft. Her eyes shining, and hungry, looking all over my face, chest, body. I'm wearing only my boxers. My cock is stiff. Her eyes keep lingering and jumping back to my face, hopeful that her punishment is over and she'll be rewarded between her legs.

I stand and take her in my arms, bringing hers to wrap around me. She melts to me, trying to bring every inch of herself in contact with me. "Thank you, Sir."

I meet her mouth arching up to mine, our kiss deep and long. She puts her hands on the top of my boxers and looks for permission with her eyes. I nod slightly and she pulls them down. I pull her onto the bed, falling back with her body on mine, stretched out together.

I roll us over, so she's pinned under my weight. Pulling myself up onto my elbows. "Open your legs...wider. Good girl." I cup her pussy, not putting a finger in, but pressing with my whole hand. "Hands by your sides." She obeys, moving her hands to be pinned between her body and my knees. I sit up and slide into her.

I can feel her moan inside, it's so deep and long. I lightly slap her face, her eyes pop open again, her pussy squeezing me. I'm grinning at her. Her confused mix of emotions plays across her face.

"You belong to me, Lucy. And I'll do whatever I like to you. *Whenever* I feel like it. Do you understand me?"

"Y...Yes, Sir." Her sweet girl voice, chin pressed down. With her arms pinned, she can't do anything to protect herself. *Good.*

"And I like slapping you. I like the look on your face..." I slap her again, just lightly, enough to shock her into automatically squeezing my cock again.

"My look...?"

I thrust in and out of her a little, her moans and wetness make stopping hard, but I finally slow down. "Yes...you have the perfect look..." I slap her again; she actually moans this time and holds the squeeze, pushing her hips against me. *God, she's gorgeous.* I have to breathe to stop from coming.

I thrust into her hard again and she pushes against me more. I give in to the desire to fuck her hard and fast. I stretch out my legs and with my arms around her, we come together quickly.

I roll off her and she instantly crawls into my arms again. I brush her hair away from her forehead and kiss the top of her head. "Your look...it's like you're begging me to stop and begging me for more all in one. What were you thinking just then…when I smacked you?"

She shyly lowers her head into my chest more and in her highest, quietest voice, "I was thinking that I wanted to please you. That if slapping me pleases you...then that's what I want too...and" she pauses for a long moment. "And I like that you do what you want to me...I like that I'm yours the way no else can ever be..."

"You are most *definitely* mine, little girl!" I smack her hip and push her onto her back so I can look at her face, into her eyes. I kiss her and her arms go around my neck, so warm, so small.

She snuggles back into my arms when I lay down again. "I want to make sure that you understand, Lucy. I'll do whatever I want to you...slap, spank, *whatever*. Always when you deserve it, for being a bad girl. But sometimes, it will be just because I want to. Do you understand that I still love you, even if I'm rough with you?"

"Yes...I love you, too, Max." She kisses my chest. "And...And I like that you're rough..." She adds this so quietly, shyly.

I say no more and feel Lucy's breathing lengthening. I turn my head so I can watch her nap for a while. *I still can't believe all that has happened between us.*

I can't believe that I've finally found a girl who can understand my tough love, my disciplinary ways. A girl who obeys my every rule...*at least tries to*, I smile...and takes the punishment she deserves when she doesn't. My heart wants to burst looking at her sweet face on my chest. *I'm a lovestruck, gushing idiot.*

I fall asleep finally, with my cheek pressed against her head.

I wake to her smile. Her face is turned up towards mine, still curled against my chest. "Can we go to the grocery store?" She says this with a secret grin.

"Okay..."

"I want to make you something special for breakfast tomorrow." She smiles bigger and jumps out of bed. Stopping though before heading to the bathroom, "If you think you'll like it that is?"

19 Him

"This is very good, baby. You're becoming a good cook." I'm downing a second helping of her croissant egg casserole. We bought everything yesterday for a recipe she downloaded, so she could make it the night before for me.

"I'm glad you like it. I found a few more recipes that you'll have to guinea pig too," she's smiling though, very proud of herself.

"As long as you don't burn it, I'll try it." She throws her napkin at me.

She's quiet though as she clears the table. I grab her hand and pull her onto my lap. "What's up? Why the quiet face?"

She shyly makes eye contact. "Have you thought more about my company picnic? ...It's next weekend...so if I'm not going to make it....I should tell some people soon..." I smile to myself that she knows asking a second time is reason enough to make me mad. But this was a pre-rule planned event, so I'm indulgent with her.

"We can go." She hugs my neck and says thank you.

"It's too bad your CEO's house isn't on the other side of the lake, we could've just driven on to my parent's tonight," I look around at the line of cars waiting for the valet. *This is going to be crowded.*

I look at Lucy. She's also staring out the window, at the large house beyond the long drive. The place is impressive. It's about three times the size of my parent's lake house. Must have at least thirteen bedrooms.

She said the party was taking place on the lawn, with the full grounds made over for team-building games, the pool and lake made into team activities too. She knew I wouldn't let her run around in a bathing suit though. She's wearing a loose cotton dress, flip flops, with her hair pulled into a messy knot at the base of her neck, no makeup. She looks perfect, smiling at me as I watch her wait for the valet to open her door.

We walk hand-in-hand up the stairs and through the open doors. Refreshments are available everywhere, trays circulating, a bar set up in a corner and outside. I hand an iced tea to Lucy and we walk through the foyer, past the winding dual staircases and elaborate mirrors.

"This place is massive." Lucy is whispering to me, looking everywhere with wide-eyes.

"I'll get ya a place like this someday," I wink at her and she hugs my arm to her side. "Maybe with a few more rooms, though..." We both laugh.

We spot Laura and Tad first and head towards a canopied area of tables set up on the lawn. "Hey you two. Welcome to the swankiest place I've ever been." Laura hugs Lucy and smiles at me. Tad shakes my hand.

"I know. I can't get over it. People actually live like this?" Lucy is watching a volleyball game a few feet away. Tracy is on the other side of the net, in a tiny red maillot with cutoff shorts over it. She sees us and waves. Lucy waves before turning back to me, facing the water. A large tile-surround pool area is dwarfed by the sparkling of Lake Michigan beyond. People are everywhere.

"We just got here too. We were about to head to the beach..." Laura obviously has a bikini on under her t-shirt and shorts. I'm glad I didn't let Lucy bring a swimsuit. This is business-fun not vacation-fun. I may not care about her work, but I do care about how she's perceived.

Lucy looks to me for direction, "Sure." She smiles at my answer and takes my hand again.

"Did you guys bring suits? The pool is amazing. It has one of those wave maker thingies in it." Laura continues talking without waiting for answers. *She's sweet, but Tad must have a lot of patience or bad hearing.*

Before we reach the pool, though, Lucy is stopped by a tall, mid-forties woman with light brown hair. I recognize her as Lucy's boss. "Catherine, it's so nice to see you." Lucy almost sounds sincere. I smile and put out my hand. The woman looks me up and down before shaking it.

"So you're the mystery guy with the private car and Cartier on call, eh?" Lucy unconsciously moves her left wrist back. I'd given her another watch to replace the one that was stolen. The face of this one is surrounded by diamonds and has an engraving, "Always."

I cock an eyebrow at the woman Lucy calls Cruela. *I can see why; she tries for intimidating.* Sitting tall in her seat, polo shirt and long crisp shorts, not feminine but not manly either, she sizes me up. "No mystery...I'm Lucy's *real* boss," I give her a wink. She only laughs, giving me an appraising look still. Lucy looks uncomfortably down at her feet. I pull her to my side more, "Have fun today," and we walk away.

With the volleyball game over, Tracy and Josh intersect our walk towards the beach. "Hey. So you do still come out to play." Tracy bumps hips with Lucy, looking at me though. "Was Cruela nice today...was that an actual smile you just got?" Josh isn't saying anything, just nods a hello. I nod back.

"She was. Max charms everybody, though." Lucy leans into me a little more, our legs in sync as we start walking again.

Tracy doesn't comment on this. "We're going to do the paddleboat races later, you guys up for it?" Lucy looks to me to answer, but Tracy just rolls her eyes, "Come on, Luce...it'll be fun. You and I can be on a team together."

"Sounds like fun...sure." I answer for us. Lucy smiles, but Tracy gives me another wary look.

We find Laura in a group of people standing in the water; she's in a white bikini, her voluptuous body on display and getting a lot of attention. Lucy looks to me and I nod her towards the water, she kicks off her shoes and heads towards Laura, with Tracy right behind, "Where's your bikini?" I sit at one of the picnic table benches set up, Josh sits next to me.

"I...I didn't bring one."

"Why not...Master wouldn't let you?" Tracy says this like she's out of a horror film, laughing. I don't hear Lucy's reply; she's standing too far with her back to me, splashing water onto her arms in long motions. The sunshine electrifies her curls, like a halo. Her dress isn't see-thru, but the outline of her legs is clearly visible. *She's beautiful.*

Josh finally says something to me, "Sorry about the other night...I don't hold grudges, ya know."

"Ancient history." I smile at him. *Not a bad guy, just young, younger than his age. He's more interested in fitting in than making his own way.*

"Cool."

I watch as the group in the water gets a little bigger. Tracy runs back to our table and takes her shorts off, kissing Josh before heading to the water again. Her one-piece is smaller than most bikinis. Her flaming hair matching its brightness. I shake my head and look sideways at Josh, who's staring off in another direction.

I'm drawn back to the water, hearing Lucy's high laughter. A guy is splashing water onto her and Laura. She's splashing back like a kid, arms full in the water. The front of her dress and hair are clinging to her. Her nipples push the thin material. She's hiding behind Laura, who's trying to push her in front of her. They stop their water fight, but my view of Lucy is blocked by the guys surrounding them.

I wait only a moment before taking off my boat shoes and moving towards the water. *She should know better than to be in a group of guys dripping wet like that!* I meet her at the water's edge, walking back with Laura.

By her look, downward-eyes and covering her chest, she knows she's in trouble. "Laura has a towel I can use," she says this quickly, not looking up at me. I follow her back to the table and put my shoes back on.

Laura digs around her bag and pulls out two towels, handing one to Lucy. She quickly wraps it around herself, pressing it into her dress, still with her eyes down. The guy who was splashing her comes over. "Sorry about getting your clothes all wet, Luce." Up close, I can tell that he's closer to my age than Lucy's. He turns to me and Josh, "Hey...I'm Rich." I shake his hand and introduce myself; Josh does the same.

"I work with Lucy in recruiting. Well, she's been trying to help my recruiters get their heads out of their asses anyway." He laughs and touches Lucy's arm. "Lucy is one of the best. I just wish I could convince Catherine to give you to me and have you working my accounting positions." Lucy darts her eyes up to me when he touches her. She freezes at the look she sees. "Hey, Bill...come over here..." Rich is yelling at a group a few feet away. A guy walks over to join us. I haven't stopped staring at Lucy, her eyes are back down.

"Lucy," He touches her arm again and she bolts her eyes up to him, "This is Bill Mont. He's my latest hire. I know that your cross-training is over with my team, but I was hoping you wouldn't mind taking Bill under your wing a little..." He's smiling at her, touching her, like he knows her really well. I feel my jaw clenching and relax with an effort and a deep breath. "I'll buy you lunch again."

Her eyes shoot straight to mine, pleading, then she takes a breath, stands a little taller and puts her hand out to the new guy, letting the towel drop to her waist. "I'd be happy to help...but Rich really is the guy to learn from. You'll do great on his team."

Laura butts in, "Lucy is just being modest. You really want to pick this girl's brain...she's waaay smarter than any of the guys!"

Rich gives Laura's shoulder a shove, "You only say that because Lucy gives your team all the best people. And we get the leftovers as accounting support."

"Damn straight." Laura is laughing, pushing him back.

Bill just smiles at Lucy, "I'm new to recruiting, so I'd really appreciate any help you can give me, Lucy. Do you have a sec now? I know it's a day off, but I'd like to act like I'm trying to impress my boss here with my drive..." He laughs and slaps Rich on the arm, "And he does talk highly about you. Do you mind?"

Lucy hesitates, still avoiding looking at me directly again, "Um...sure...how can I help?"

And this guy actually turns away from me. Puts his hand on Lucy's arm. And tries to take two steps away from me with her. Lucy is already turning back to me, when I step in. I grab both of her arms from behind, not squeezing, only holding her firmly. "*I* mind, Bill."

The guy blinks at me, everyone is quiet. I see Tracy out of the corner of my eye has joined the group again too. Her mouth is wide open. Laura is looking embarrassed. The guy is backing off, "Oh...sorry...I, um, didn't mean any..."

Rich butts in, "It's supposed to be a party. Just have fun, Bill, you'll have plenty of time to impress me in the office." He laughs, but he's looking at Lucy, concerned.

Lucy's head is bent down slightly, her eyes completely averted. I haven't let go of her. I let her pull her arms away to bring the towel around to her front finally. She continues drying off more. Rich makes a quick good-bye, saying he'll see Lucy in the office next week and takes Bill with him. Tracy gives a look to Josh and he walks off.

"Lucy, you wanna tell me why every guy here thinks he can put his hands on you?" My voice is steady, the deep warning one she knows so well. Lucy shrinks more and starts to answer me.

"What the fuck, Max?!" Tracy is in my face. She's tall, but only comes up to my chin. She's moved to be between Lucy and me.

Lucy grabs Tracy's arm. "Please...keep your voice *down.* People are looking..." Laura also looks around and stands closer to Lucy.

"Answer me, Lucy."

Her eyes meet mine as she steps in front of Tracy again, drawn to me. "I'm sorry, Si...Max."

Tracy grabs Lucy's arm and twists her around to face her. "Why are *you* saying you're sorry? *He* should be sorry for making you look like some spineless wimp in front of Rich!"

I ignore Tracy and take hold of the back of Lucy's arms again. She almost falls into my chest, her body yielding to my touch and voice. "Is *that* how you answer me?"

Her face turns to the side, chin up, eyes looking up into mine again; she swallows hard. Tracy and Laura just stare. "I'm sorry...Sir." She almost whispers this, the pleading in her eyes stronger than her voice.

"What the fuck?!" Tracy is trying to pull at Lucy's hand, but I have hold of both of her arms. "Snap out of it! Why are you doing this?"

Laura pulls Tracy's arm back and whispers angrily, "Stop it. People *are* looking." But she's also staring in disbelief at Lucy.

Tracy takes a deep breath and looks around. Quieter this time, "Why are you letting him push you around like this?"

"He's not. I was wrong to let them touch me. ...It was disrespectful."

"Disrespectful to you? Or to *him*?" Tracy shoots me another hard look.

My face is calm, only a slight furrow to my brow. "Both," I answer for Lucy.

Tracy is again staring at me like she wants to tell me off, but she turns her eyes back down to Lucy, in a calmer voice, "You don't need this guy. He's been way too controlling all along and he's gone too far..."

"I..." Lucy stops, tears starting to make her voice shake, "I like...how controlling Max is...and it's none of your business." My pride in her matches my anger.

"What the...I don't even *know* what to say to you right now!" Tracy is just shaking her head, arms crossed, glaring at us. Laura has a shocked look, dragging her eyes from Lucy to me and back. "Lucy...you need to get your head out of your ass. He's a control freak and you shouldn't be with him." Tracy glares for another second, waiting for her to respond. Lucy is shaking, but silent against me. "If you stay with him...you're an idiot." Tracy turns and stomps off. Laura only looks from Lucy to me one more time and turns to run after Tracy.

We stand with her back against me for a moment longer. I let go of one of her arms and squeeze the other a little harder. She doesn't say anything, just keeps up as I walk us quickly back towards the house.

Inside, I head up the stairs. Lucy hesitates on the first step, but I pull her along and she quickly keeps pace. I pass several rooms before going in one that looks like an unused guest room. I shove Lucy inside and close the door behind me.

With my hand still on the door, my back to her, "Now. Do you wanna tell me why every guy here thinks he can touch you?" I turn and she's shivering in the middle of the room. She only shakes her head until I walk to stand in front of her, towering over her.

"I...I don't know, Max...I'm sorry...please!"

"That's not an answer, Lucy."

"Because....because..." She's starting to hiccup, her breathing out of control. She takes a deep breath and tries to steady herself.

"Because you *have* been disrespectful, haven't you?" She only shakes her head slightly, "Oh...you haven't? You weren't just running around with your dress soaked, laughing and playing with some guy...the same guy who thinks he can put his hand on you and take you to lunch?!"

She starts to cry, choking out, "I'm sorry, Sir," wrapping her arms around her middle to hide how her dress still clings.

"No. No tears, little girl." She looks up and swallows back her next sob. I give her a moment to calm again. "You'll have *plenty* to cry about." Her beautiful eyes fill with fear. This is the angriest I've been with her. I haven't yelled, but she knows she's in for a punishment. I'm trying to keep control of my anger, but I can feel myself heating up.

"Take off your dress."

Her eyes dart to the door, in quiet fear, "Here?!"

I slap her, not too hard. I'm glad that I'm still in control of my anger enough to stop from slapping her as hard as I want to. Her hand goes up to her face. "I tell you to do something, you do it. No questions. I thought you knew *that* lesson at least, Lucy. Looks like I need to review *all* the rules with you."

She shakes her head and pulls off her dress quickly. "No...No, Sir...I'm sorry, Sir...I didn't mean..."

When she's standing in only her bra and thong, I take off my belt. Her eyes follow my hands, saucers of fear; she's frozen. "Stand by the bed." I nod behind her. A nice four-poster bed takes up most of the rest of the room.

She moves awkwardly, her feet tripping a little. "Put your hands up on the post." She does. "On tip-toe." She stretches up. Her back and arm muscles are taut. Her calves harden. Her tiny thong doesn't cover her cheeks at all.

"Why are you being punished, Lucy?" I can barely grit out the words through my grinding teeth.

"Because..." She has to swallow several times before she can finish, "Because I let two men touch me and....and I questioned you."

"And..." She is unable to answer, just shakes on the post.

"You acted indecently, didn't you?"

"Yes, Sir...I...I was indecent in the water...with other men around."

"And..." Again she's unable to answer. Her body shakes with unshed tears, her forehead pressed against the post.

"And you've gone to lunch with a man I don't know...without my *permission*..." She tries to say something, but I cut her off. "You seem to have the hardest time with this lesson, Lucy..." I say this sadly, almost tenderly.

She sobs once, but quickly gulps back any more. She chokes on her apology, only getting out, "...Sir..."

"I'm going to help you remember, little girl. I'm going to make sure that you don't *ever* forget this lesson again."

I whip the belt across her lower cheeks and upper thighs. She cries out, pressing her face into her arms. I whip twice more rapidly on the same spot. The belt mark flares up. I don't wait. The next two hit only her thighs, in rapid fire, more strangled screams. Two more marks form.

I pause to allow her breathing to get under control again, her feet to stop dancing. Her hands are clutching the post. I swallow back some of my anger, breathing a little harder myself. My anger is only fueled with spanking her, hearing her cries.

I'm not worried about anyone hearing us. The door is locked, the party is loud outside, with only staff milling about downstairs. We won't be disturbed.

"How many do you deserve, little girl?" I choke this out through gritted teeth.

She knows I mean how many times she's broken the rule. She gasps out, "Seven, Sir." Seven times she allowed a man to touch her, went behind my back out with another man. *Seven*. I see only red for a moment. I close my eyes and breathe deeply three times.

"You have two more coming then." The anger makes my voice even colder. "And one for questioning." She is shaking harder, her hand slipping on the post. She quickly reaches up and grabs it again. "Count."

I hit the tender spot again. The mark goes white. Her feet dance and her cries are high-pitched yelps. She mouths more than says, "One," into her arms.

I hit once more on her thigh, making the other two marks meet. She strangles this cry, "Tt...two..."

My last one is aimed a little lower on her thigh. I haven't hit her here before. She cries out again, her voice raw. Finally, squeaking out, "Three."

I don't let her catch her breath. I grab the back of her head by her hair, pulling her off the post and shoving her down on the floor. She crawls and rolls over. On my knees, I grab her legs and yank them out, pulling her towards me. She cries out as the belt marks flare from the carpet. I smile.

"Please...please, Max...I'm sorry..."

"Hands behind your head." She immediately obeys.

I tear her thong off. She whimpers, but stays quiet. Shoving three fingers into her wet pussy, I lean over her. "Who does this belong to?"

"It belongs to you...I belong to you!"

I take my fingers out to the tips and shove them back, my knuckle meeting her bone. "Again."

"I belong to you!"

"Again."

"I belong to you!" I do this seven times. She's crying, eyes closed, but she keeps her hands behind her head. Her cries only drive me to want to hurt her more. I stop and take a few deep breaths, she keeps her eyes closed still.

I pull off my shorts. Grabbing her knees, I bend her legs up, pressing her thighs wide and back. I shove inside her deep. She cries out again. I know from this angle, I'm able to go deeper than she likes. I stay inside, not moving. Her eyes finally open.

"You went behind my back *seven* times with other men?"

She starts to shake her head, bringing her elbows to both sides protectively, "...No...No...Max...I only went to lunch...once...it was a team...a work thing...I swear..."

"And you let guys touch you." I say this quietly, staring down at her in angry disbelief.

She moans, a wounded animal, "I'm sorry...I won't let...I won't ever let anyone touch me again...I swear, Max...please...please forgive me." She's crying uncontrollably again.

I pull out and shove in deep again, her sobs are interrupted with a stronger moan. I fuck her hard, in and out, deep, my body pressing on her legs, the carpet burning her ass. We come together, both of us crying out.

I sit back and Lucy rolls onto her side, crying, sobbing a "thank you." The belt marks on her thighs are a deep red with a few bumps, the tender spot is a raised welt with swollen edges. I slap her hip. "Get up. We're leaving."

I pull up my shorts, grab her torn underwear and put it in my pocket. I head to the bathroom. When I come out, Lucy is unsteady on her feet, pulling up her dress. She doesn't look at me.

"Go to the bathroom...wipe your face and clean up." She moves numbly by me.

My anger is only slightly spent. I am hurt by her betrayals. My anger keeps heating up and I have to breathe deeply to get it under control again.

When she comes out of the bathroom, she is still shy and pleading with her eyes. I put my hand out to her and she quickly runs into my arms. She's still crying softly and begging my forgiveness.

"Shhh, baby...it's okay...I love you...shhh..." But I'm still seeing red. She finally quiets and I open the door.

20 Her

Max keeps his hand on my lower back, rubbing a small spot made raw from the carpet, but I know better than to move away from him. I feel my ass burning under my dress, the very bottom almost numb with pain. My swollen and sore pussy pulls between my legs as I walk, with no underwear to keep from hurting more. We move quickly down the stairs and out the doors. My only relief is not running into anyone I know. *I have no idea what I would do if Tracy confronted me now.*

I wait by the curb while he tips the valet. Max opens my door and watches as I gently lower myself onto the seat. He gives me one last hard look before going to his side and getting in. He races down the drive.

I try to find a comfortable position on the seat. My lower bottom sits directly on the leather and I can't get away from the added pain. "Sit still." His voice has a ragged edge, a deep ember to it.

He doesn't look at me, but turns on the cooling fans for my seat. I quietly say, "Thank you," as I feel the small relief. *But now I have a long drive, with no ability to reposition.* I'll be lucky if I can walk when we get home, my whole body is so tense.

This thought makes me cry, that I could make Max this angry with me, this disappointed.

"No. No more tears. You just sit there and think about what you've done." I sniffle and try not to cry. Soon, my eyes burn as much as my ass.

I can't help reliving how the day started to how it ended. *And it's all my fault! If I hadn't been indecent, if I hadn't let those men touch me, if I hadn't gone to lunch without permission...none of this would have happened.* I berate myself in silence, stealing glances at Max when I can. His face remains statue, the angry God in his beauty, his jaw firm and eyes narrowed.

When we pull into his garage spot, I know a new fear though. This is the first time that his anger has extended past disciplining me. *I don't know that I can take more punishment.*

He opens the door and gives me both arms to help me up. "Go slow." I glance at his face, his voice was deceptively tender, his expression is still stony. My thighs are knotted, my ass swollen and stiff. I move slowly towards the elevators, holding his arm more for comfort than support on the ride up. It's the most he's touched me since we left the party.

As soon as his door closes behind him, he orders me to undress. I don't hesitate. The cool air feels good on my backside. But I shake from fear not coldness. "Face the wall, Lucy." I pivot into position. Praying for his mercy, but knowing I don't deserve any. I want to cry, but keep my tears bottled.

"Begin."

His shortness and disappointment hurt as much as my bodily pain. I recite again all of my transgressions.

"Again."

He makes me repeat everything seven times. My voice is hoarse from holding in tears. His voice doesn't lose any of its anger.

He paces behind me. I want so much to put my arms around him, but I don't move, keeping my head up the way he likes. *I no longer fear the pain...I fear no release from this torture...knowing that I've hurt him and he can't forgive me...that he won't be able to make me his good girl again.* I shudder a breath in and hold it as long as I can.

I speak quietly, a little calmer. "Please...forgive me...please."

He stops pacing, right behind me. "I want to. I can't stop thinking about your betrayal. You let men touch you and treat you like...like a *whore*, Lucy. Like *they* could have you, when you *belong* to me." His voice is broken, raw with his anger.

"Then...then punish me...please. Anything so you can forgive me. So I can deserve your forgiveness. ...I can't take you not loving me."

"I love you very much." His voice is almost back to tender again. I can't stop a tear from sliding down my cheek. "But I can't punish you more...not tonight. You are too swollen already." Knowing that he's putting my safety and care ahead of his anger, even in his darkness, tortures me more. "I keep pacing hoping my anger will subside, but all I want to do is take my belt to you until I can't picture your betrayals anymore." He says this with such sadness, but the anger is still there. He starts pacing again.

With my arms firmly behind my back, I lower myself slowly onto my knees, still facing the wall. I'm completely numb, unable to feel the strain that my legs and butt must be under with this motion. "Max...please...I'll do anything to deserve your forgiveness." I lower my head and take a deep breath. "Do...do what you have to do...punish me...*please*!" And I know that I mean this. That I would take his slaps and belt, anything so long as he would forgive me. That I would trust my body to his care completely in order to have his loving forgiveness again.

He walks away. *To get the belt himself.* I try to steady my breathing, knowing that I'll need every breath to get through this. When he returns, I stiffen, feeling the pain in my legs and butt momentarily. I breathe out slowly, raise my head, and close my eyes.

But it's not the belt I feel. It's cool and silky. Max binds my wrists with one of his ties, next my ankles. I panic for a second, trying to swallow and breathe. *I can't move and he's going to beat me like this.* I lower my head only slightly in an agony of shame. *He doesn't even trust me not to move.*

He steps back and I brace myself. "I made a promise to you, little girl." I want so badly to see his face, because his voice is unreadable...not quite tender, not quite angry, not quite sad...and all of them at once. "I promised not to hurt you so badly that you wouldn't heal and..." He pauses for a full minute. "And if I start punishing you again tonight I may not be able to keep that promise." He picks me up, my arms pinned painfully underneath me. I look into his eyes, but he won't meet mine. He walks into the bedroom and goes straight to the closet. He stops in front of the door and finally looks at me.

The pain I see breaks my heart. He's searching my face, looking for an answer. I feel only shame and beg with my eyes for his forgiveness. He opens the door with one hand and lowers me to the carpet, on my side.

"You'll sleep here tonight. Think about what you've done. No more tears, though. You don't get to cry yourself to sleep, little girl." And he closes the door, leaving me in darkness. I gasp. *I can't believe he's leaving me here...without...without any release from his torture!*

I don't move. I concentrate on my breathing to steady myself. I can see a sliver of light under the door and hear small movements. Max walks around the bedroom. I don't know how long I stare at that light, my only ray of hope that he'll come back in here, take me in his arms. *Love me or beat me...just do something.* My eyes begin to burn again; a tear crab walks down my cheek to the carpet. I blink several times to stop more from joining it

Max doesn't want me to cry. And I desperately want to earn his forgiveness, not make him more disappointed and angry. I stay awake, not moving, only breathing, staring at that light. I don't know how long this goes on.

Finally, the light goes off and I'm in full darkness. I can hear Max getting in bed. I don't hear his steady breathing. I don't feel his chest hairs on my cheek. I don't feel his hand in my hair, lulling me into sweet dreams. I only feel the rough carpet and I pretend it's his touch. I don't know when I sleep, when my fevered prayers for his forgiveness finally give way to dreams as fevered.

21 Him

Her eyes blink to the light, as I stand over her. She hasn't moved all night, except small twitches and moans from bad dreams that I could hear from my side of the door. I didn't sleep at all.

I squat down and untie her ankles, then her wrists. I stop her from sitting up though. "Move your arms first. Before you sit up." Her look is hopeful to my tenderness. I help her sit, holding her upper body. She has to sit sideways, her ass still swollen and raw, her thighs not as bad.

I pick her up under her arms and help her to the bed. She sits softly on the edge. I have a glass of water for her and make her take a sip. "I have to use the bathroom." Her lips and throat are dry.

"Ask me." My abruptness changes her hopeful look into fear and shame again.

"Please...may I go to the bathroom, Sir?"

"Who does your body belong to Lucy?" She blinks for only a second.

"You, Sir."

"I own you." I say this flatly.

"Yes...Yes, Sir."

"Say it."

"You own me, Max." She pleads to me, with a look of love, longing, lust. "You own me. Max, you own me...you own me...please...you own me...you own me..."

I hush her with a kiss. And quietly, "I own every part of you, Lucy. You don't even have the right to decide when you pee, unless I give you that right. Do you understand that?"

"Yes, Sir!"

"Go make breakfast." She moves slowly off the bed and heads towards the door. "Lucy." She turns to me. "You may use the bathroom first."

"Thank you, Sir." She quietly walks to the bathroom and I follow her. I take aspirin out and walk back to the bed. When she returns I make her take these with the water. We have a long drive today and I don't want her too stiff to go.

I watch her make breakfast, quickly moving around the kitchen. Bending over with some obvious stiffness, her ass a mess of redness and bumps. *But so beautiful.*

Last night, I didn't have complete control of my anger. *I've been afraid of that, losing control like that.* I feared not being able to pull myself back from the edge of darkness, back from the violence I knew with my mom.

I've questioned If I'd be able to stop my anger long enough to keep Lucy safe. *From me.*

I realized that it's what has been holding us back. *I've been holding us back.* I've given Lucy many rules, threatened her with punishments, even spanked her a little. But always in the back of my mind, I've wondered what would happen if I lost it. If I saw red and really wanted to hurt her for angering me, disobeying me.

Last night, I proved to myself that I can reign in my anger, that I can keep as strong of a control of myself as I can of her. My desire to keep her safe is as strong as my desire to punish her, to control her, to own her.

I realized something else last night, in the darkness, feeling her absence in my bed, her soft moans tearing into my heart. I don't want only part of her. I want everything. I demand everything. I don't want to hold back anymore. I don't need to.

Today, I'll start her new lessons...

"I know you know that how you *behave* is important to me." She stops mid-air with her fork, lowering it and looking at her hands, only nodding so she doesn't interrupt. "How you *think* is equally important to me, Lucy." She looks into my eyes, trying to tell me how ashamed she is. "What lesson did you learn last night...by yourself?"

"I...I learned how badly I'd betrayed you..." She doesn't look at me, only her hands. I'd allowed her a small pillow, so she sits higher in her seat, with her hair down around her, her nipples just above the table's edge, her cheeks swollen and tear-stained still; her beauty takes my breath away. "That I will never betray you again!"

"Go on."

"I learned that I never want to make you so angry again. So angry that you can't find a way to make me your good girl...to forgive me. That I didn't deserve your forgiveness."

"Good. Because you won't be walking the next day from the spanking you'll deserve if you ever let another man touch you again. Do you understand me?" And I know now that I can take my anger to that level, that Lucy will accept it as her punishment. And that I'll be able to stop myself from going too far. I can keep her safe even from my own anger.

"Yes, Sir."

"I need you to understand something else." I take her hand from her lap and hold it in mine. Her puppy-wants-a-treat look makes me smile for a second. "I don't mean I want you to *think* about your behavior more." A little confusion crosses her face. "I mean that I want to get you to a point that your thoughts are automatically centered on me. And nothing else. And that your behavior is second nature." She nods. "Even alone in your own thoughts, I demand your obedience. I want to own you mind, body, and soul, Lucy."

"You do!" I smile at this. *I know she thinks this is true...but she has quite a few lessons before I know it will be true.*

"You better eat something. We have a long day, little girl." She obediently picks up her fork and starts eating again, smiling at me as I still hold her hand.

22 Her

This drive is so pretty, miles of trees, sunshine and peeks at the lake. The houses get bigger, the land spreads more. I recognize this area. *We should be at his parents' house soon.* This trip is so different from the last; I feel a flutter in my stomach. I'm excited and nervous.

Excited because I can't wait to show his dad how much I love Max. Ron had asked me that question last time. *This time I hope he'll be able to see that I do. And I hope to make up for everything to Max, to be on my very best behavior, so he'll be nothing but happy with me.*

I squeeze his hand on my knee. Max smiles at me again, raising his hand to my face and squeezing both my cheeks gently. I've been getting him to give me little looks and touches for the whole drive. He seems to understand that I need his constant attention. *After last night, I don't want to be without it ever again.*

Nervous...well, that's obvious... Ron is very intimidating. I know how much Max looks up to him. *And I really want him to like me, to think that I'm good enough for his son.* I've never really cared about what a guy's parents thought of me before. I know that it's important to Max, so it's important to me.

And of course, I'm nervous that Max will make these next few days a test of my obedience to him. I want so much to please him, but I'm still afraid of making him angry. *My as...my* butt *can't take much more.*

I smile, squeezing Max's arm. I know he'd be proud of me if I told him that I just stopped myself from cursing. This is what he wants. *What he said he demands.* That even in my own thoughts, I'm his good girl. He leans over and I give him a kiss on his cheek, he hugs my face to his, still looking at the road.

I can't believe how happy I am. *And with a sore bottom.* My thighs are more strained from Max pushing on them than the belt, but my butt is raw where I sit, it still throbs. Max gave me a small cushion for the car seat, but this only helps a little.

The drive is long, but I'm grateful for it. Even though I know I'll be stiff and sorer when we get there, I'm glad to have this time to think. Everything went downhill so fast yesterday, that I haven't had a chance to think about it. Now that it's over, I can.

Max was so angry; I still can't believe I was that stupid. I felt this almost out of body thing. I saw myself doing the things that I knew would make him angry, acting like I could do whatever I please. But I didn't know why.

Last night, in the closet, I kept reliving everything. Going over and over it all.

I felt this tug-of-war between what my co-workers and friends expect of me and what Max expects of me. I just went into auto-mode and acted like I do at work, around Tracy and Laura. Last night, just before falling asleep, I realized that this is when I get into trouble. When I ignore that Max expects me to be his good girl all the time, no matter what, and I try to get away with being my old self.

But my old self didn't have this.

I steal a guilty look at him. He only picks up my hand and kisses it, making me smile again. "I'm sorry about yesterday, Max."

He looks surprised. "Is that what has you so quiet? You're thinking about yesterday still?"

"..Yes..." I still feel guilty.

"Well...stop. That's an order!" He kisses my hand again and winks at me.

"But... Can I say one more thing, Sir?"

His smile gets bigger. "Yes, you may..."

"I was bad on purpose!" I blurt this out. He looks sideways at me quickly before pulling his eyes back to the road. "I mean...not on purpose exactly. But I...I wanted to pretend that I could get away with acting like that. That just because I was around my friends...and co-workers," I say this part extra quiet, extra guilty, "that it was an excuse."

"Go on." I'm beginning to feel that knot again. *Why did I start this conversation? We were having such a pleasant drive.* He kisses my hand again. "You are a very good girl for telling me. Go on."

"I realized last night...on the floor that I...I wouldn't have been happy if you'd let me get away with it. If the excuse had been okay with you..."

He smiles again. "You don't have any excuse for disobedience, Lucy. Ever." I smile at this too.

No, my old self didn't have someone who cares so much about me, loves me as much as I love him.

23 Him

"You didn't forget the presents, right?" It's the second time Lucy's asked me.

"No, baby. They're in the trunk." I laugh as she fidgets with her hands. She's been needy all morning. Doing little things to get my attention, to draw my hands to her. I give her reassurance again, squeezing both her hands in her lap. She smiles at me.

I'm impressed that she was able to see her own actions so clearly yesterday. I knew that she was testing her limits. Seeing what she could get away with. But the fact that she could see it too, and see that she didn't want me to let her get away with anything. *Well, I'm a lucky man to have such a good girl!*

This second trip to my folks is a family tradition. An end of summer, closing of the lake house, although not officially, annual event. We've even spent Christmas up here before. It's a little soon after our last trip here, but I'll be happy to show off Lucy. She's come so far in such a short time.

She's so much more confident in her place with me. She understands what I expect. She's grown in her ability to stand up for us. The talks with Jake and Dan were big helps. She was able to say that she was fine with my disciplining her. *Not the full, shout from the roof kinda thing, but I'll take it for now.*

I know she's ignored all calls and texts from Tracy and Laura. *I'll have to make her deal with them sooner or later, before the end of our visit.* My friends and family accept me, her, us. Hers need to do the same or no longer be counted as friends. *I need to push her on this point. She's ready.*

And after yesterday, I know that I can push her on anything. I believed that before, but now I know it's true. I hit her hard with the belt. I took my anger out on her, but I stayed in control. I smile to myself. *Although I imagined hitting her twenty more times.* I gave her a just punishment, and she took it. She accepted that she deserved it. And she's better for it.

Lucy was excited about coming up again so soon. We're going to spend three days. I made her take off Tuesday to make the long weekend even longer. She insisted on shopping and getting presents for both my parents, as a thank you for their hospitality this time and last.

I smile as she squeezes my hand again. *Such a needy girl today.*

I open the car door and help Lucy out, just as Mom is walking out the front door. Lucy is stiff from sitting for so long, but she embraces my mom with a big hug.

"Mrs. Traeger...I mean, Alex! It's so good to see you again."

"Lucy, it's good to see you, too." Mom keeps her arm around Lucy's shoulders. She's almost a head taller than her. Lucy is dressed in a plain white dress with short sleeves, soft and loose. The dress reaches just below her knees, covering the marks on her thighs.

I lean in and kiss Mom on the cheek; she hugs me with her free arm. "Where's Dad?"

"He had to go into town for a bit. I forgot some things back at the house and he had a few errands to run. He should be back any minute." Mom turns Lucy towards the house.

"I'll grab the bags and be right in."

Lucy turns at the first step up, "You'll bring *all* the bags in?"

I only roll my eyes at her, "Yes...go inside." She immediately turns and follows my mom, who waited by the front doors. Mom notices how slow and stiff Lucy is on the stairs, but says nothing. She only smiles at me.

Dad pulls up just as I'm setting our bags on the gravel drive. He walks over, setting a grocery bag down and hugs me. "Glad you could make it up this weekend, Max."

"Me, too. Sorry we couldn't be here yesterday. I let Lucy go to her company's picnic up in Michigan. We made good time getting here today though." I open the passenger door to grab Lucy's purse; Dad notices the pillow on her seat, but doesn't say anything.

We walk together up the stairs, hearing Mom and Lucy in the kitchen, laughing.

Lucy is leaning over the counter. Ron sets the bag of groceries on the island. They were probably only apart for thirty minutes, but Mom rushes to be in his arms and kiss him hello again. Lucy smiles watching them.

"Put the groceries away, Lucy." *I intend to order her around a lot this weekend.*

She startles for a second, unsure of where everything would go I'm sure, but immediately starts taking everything out of the bag and placing it on the counter. "Do you put your onions in the fridge, Alex?" I smile that she's being on her best behavior. Dad winks at me.

"No...There's a bin in the pantry. Yes, just down one shelf is for the onions. Thank you, sweetie." Mom smiles at me too. "Now. All men out of my kitchen... I have lunch to prepare." She shoos us out with her apron. "Lucy, you can help me with the pie for tonight."

Dad and I head out to the terrace. The landscape is already changing, the waves are higher and the beach is smaller, rockier. Every spring, they have to repair the retaining wall after a harsh winter. Today it's still warm and the water in the air is sweet; thunderclouds are just rolling in.

Lucy comes out with two beers and hands each of us one. She laughs and rubs the top of my head, "Your mom was just telling me that you've never liked peas. She couldn't get you to eat them either." Lucy is learning my likes and dislikes. Not all of what she's made has been good, but she's improving.

Dad answers, "Max was a picky eater as a kid. At least he *tried* to be." He tips his beer at me and laughs.

"I went to bed many a night with an empty stomach and a sore butt." I laugh too. Lucy winces when I squeeze my arm around her hips. Her own butt is still very sore. "Lucy's becoming a good cook."

"I want to make breakfast for all of us tomorrow. If that's okay with you, Mr. Tra...Ron?" The only way I could've been prouder of her is if she'd called him sir.

Dad smiles at us, looking from me to Lucy, "Of course, Lucy. That'll be very nice. It'll give Alex a break. But she'll probably be snooping around trying to help, just so you know." He winks at her. She relaxes against my arm.

"I can use all the help I can get. I'm still burning toast." She laughs at herself and heads back into the kitchen.

"She seems...happier...this time," Dad is watching me as I follow Lucy with my eyes. Her hips are just visible under her loose dress, her hair sways with her pretty walk, one foot in front of the other. She knows I'm watching her.

"She is." I take a swig of beer and change the subject. "Have you talked to Jake?"

"Yes. He called yesterday. Finally."

"Good. He still won't return my calls..."

"I know. He says he needs a little time." Dad looks down at the bottle cradled in his hands. "He told me that his split with Julia is a good thing though, so maybe he's coming around. Have some faith."

I sigh, "I will. But I'm not going to give up trying to reach him."

"I wouldn't expect you to." He tips his beer to me again and takes a deep drink.

Lucy comes back out, "Alex says lunch is ready. Where would you like to eat, Ron?"

Dad gives her a big smile. "Looks like it might actually rain. We can eat inside, Lucy." He gives me a big smile too, as Lucy walks away. "She's definitely different..."

"Lucy will clean up, Mom." Mom stops from picking up plates, looking at Dad. Lucy just looks at me for a second, before jumping up and taking the plates from her. Dad puts his arm out and Mom steps into it, out of Lucy's way.

"Why don't you get a game ready for us, Max? The weather's perfect for a good ass-kicking." Ron is rubbing his hands together. He's always loved being in this house during a storm, all of us around to play games.

We head into the family room while Mom heads into the kitchen with Lucy. She doesn't do anything, just tells Lucy where everything is. *She knows better than to interfere with an order I've given to Lucy.*

24 Her

"Your kitchen is huge, Alex." I'm just finishing with the last pot, ready to dry, the dishwasher humming along quietly. "It's so beautiful too."

"Thank you. Ron picked out every detail; I think it's where Jake got his interest in architecture. Ron's always been involved in the planning and building of all of our homes." She obviously has a lot of pride. Everything is spotless and neatly put away. She's been able to tell me where everything goes from her spot on the counter stool.

I know Max wanted me to do this, so I'm glad that Alex didn't try to help me, other than give some directions on how not to scratch her copper pots.

"My mom always wanted to build a home. But she and my dad never moved when I was a kid. And now they're in a townhome. It's new and she's made it her own. But nothing like this."

"What part of Arizona are your folks in, Lucy?" *Max must have talked about my family to her.* That thought makes me smile as I answer.

"Near Sedona." I'm busy polishing the last pot with the towel. *I want Max to notice that everything shines.*

"It must be hard for you...that they're so far away..."

"It was at first. They've been out there for a little while now, and my brother, PJ, and his family are still around here. So, it's not so bad."

"Yes. But a girl should have her mother and father near..." Her tone has changed slightly, more cautious. I don't know why though. "Did you think about moving out there?" I hang the pot back in its place and stop to match her appraising look.

"No. I have a life, job, here. I was only just starting on my career after college, but I couldn't just leave. Besides, I think my dad wanted the retirement life...all play, no worries for a little while." I'm trying to lighten the mood, shrugging and moving to sit next to her on a stool. I have to sit carefully, so as not to land hard on my butt. I lean forward on the counter, taking the pressure off of my sorest spot; I've had to sit on it for too long already.

She continues looking at me strangely though, turning to face me on her stool, before finally asking, "Would you still choose your job...over being close to family?"

"I...I don't think it matters anymore. They're happy and I'm happy...here...with Max." I'm not sure what she's getting at, but I'm starting to feel a knot in my stomach, waiting for the punchline.

"*Are* you happy with Max?" Her look remains piercing.

I was expecting this from Ron, not her. "Yes." I don't want to elaborate.

She keeps going anyway, "And if he asked you to choose family over your job...?"

The punchline. I swallow, looking at my knees. *No use beating around the bush.* I answer quietly, "We both know that Max wouldn't be *asking* me anything..."

She smiles, the first sign of her look thawing, "No. I suppose not..."

I look her directly in the eye, "And I'd choose Max over anything."

Her smile warms even more, her hand rests on my arm on the counter, "Good. I'm glad to hear that." She squeezes my arm and gets up to move around the kitchen. She starts taking things out of the pantry and refrigerator. "I suppose Max told you that Ron adopted him and Jake?" I only nod, waiting to see where she's taking this conversation again. "Ron's a good man. He's been a very good father to both our boys."

She moves quickly around, pulling plates and glasses. I can't believe after the big lunch, she thinks anyone is going to be hungry enough to eat the snacks she's preparing. I just watch as she pours tea into a pitcher and puts everything on two trays. She finally stops and looks at me again. "Ron's a *very* traditional man...and he's raised our boys to be the same." I nod cautiously to this. "I suppose Max has told you all this already...?" I nod the same. "Good." She pauses, turning back to the trays, "Good."

But she stops in front of me once more, the counter between us now. "I'm glad to see Max so happy, Lucy. He's a good man, too." She has a tear in her voice, and her eyes shine.

I reach across and take her hand. "I want to make Max very happy, Alex." I want her to know that Max means the world to me.

She smiles and squeezes my hand, wiping her eyes on her apron, "We better get these in there...games always make Ron hungry." I pick up the other tray and follow her into the family room; the sound of loud laughter and play arguing over some game move being illegal meets us.

The nights are already cooler. I wrap the wool throw from the bed around my shoulders and stare over the lake. With no other noise, the sound of the waves comes straight across the lawn. I can't see them, but I know that they're high over the dock tonight. The storm passed earlier and the sky is still clearing, a few bright stars peek out from above.

I'm waiting for Max to come upstairs. He sent me to bed an hour ago at 11:00 to get ready. I thought it was funny at first. I felt strange thinking that his dad and mom would know that I was getting ready for sex with their son. I'm still not used to how comfortable they are with us sharing a room in their home. When my mom asked about our visit last time, she didn't ask where I slept and I didn't say.

After waiting so long in my pretty negligee, though, I wonder if he just wanted to give me a bedtime in front of them. *He ordered me around so much today!* I knew he would challenge me. I was jumping up constantly to do something that he said or to stop doing something that he said. *It was exhausting.* But I know that I made him happy. His smile all day was just for me, because of me. *I hope he was happy with me at least...*

I snuggle the wrap more. The night is beginning to get to me, the short pink nightie I have on under isn't much against the lake breeze.

I turn and see Max watching me from the bed. I didn't even hear him come in. He smiles and puts his hand out and I run into his arms, dropping the wrap around his shoulders to cover us both.

He smells of rich cigars and richer brandy. I love the taste of his lips, the feel of them on my neck. His hands go straight to my bottom and squeeze. I squeak in pain, but he only squeezes harder. I just hold onto his head, his lips buried between my tits. I know he likes to hear my moans, both in pain and pleasure. He pinches the very spot that hurts the most and I cry out.

He lifts his head and grins at me. "You were a very good girl today."

"Thank you, Sir." He still pinches and squeezes though. My eyes are starting to water, but I blink back any tears.

"I'm glad you told me that you acted up yesterday on purpose." *Uh-oh...I could be in trouble here.* I start to shake my head a little. "Yes. I knew you did. But I'm glad that you knew it too. I won't punish you more for it...this time." He gives an extra hard squeeze and I gasp, letting his arms hold me up more than my own legs. "But don't ever be a bad girl on purpose again, Lucy...or I *will* punish you every night for a week afterwards. Do you understand me, little girl?"

"Yes! Yes, Sir!" I know he means it. *The very thought is enough for me to never ever think about doing anything on purpose to ever make him angry ever again ever.*

He finally lets go of my bottom and kisses me, his hands going up my back. I kiss back so hard, so eager. "Now, let me see my pretty girl."

I smile and take a step back, he drops his arms and I take one more step back before lowering the wrap, but only to my shoulders, keeping it tight around me. I smile at his look, not quite stern, not quite smiling. I want to tease him a little. *He's made me wait for him; he can wait to see me.* I want to delay this moment as long as I can.

I take another step back and let the wrap fall just a little more, revealing the tiny straps of the nightie. I take another step; the lacy top is exposed. Another step, I let the wrap fall. I'm closer to the open terrace doors. The breeze pushes the nightie and my hair forward, a pink and blonde cloud around me. I only smile and wait for him to say something.

"Come here."

I take one step towards him, one foot in front of the other. "Do you like it?"

"Yes. Now get over here." He's smiling, but his voice has just a bit of edge to it.

One step, "You *really* like it?" I'm smiling and trying not to laugh, trying to look sexy.

He reaches for my hand and grabs me, yanking me back into his arms so quickly, I cry out. "Yes, I *really* like it!" He grabs the straps and pulls the nightie down in one quick movement, making me cry out again. "But I much prefer you naked."

He picks me up just under my butt with his strong arms; the pain is there but distant to my desire for him. He turns and drops me gently onto the bed and undresses. I watch his chest and arms flex. He's on me and in me so quickly I barely have my legs spread. I wrap them around his waist when he pulls out a little, looking at me.

I smile up at him, my hands on his shoulders. Although my thighs are sore, I use my legs and pull my hips up and him in. He moans. I let go of the pressure on my thighs and together we slide back down onto the bed more. "Nice trick." He moves suddenly, grabs my wrists and holds me down, slamming into my wet pussy hard. I cry out. "Is that what you wanted, little girl?"

"Yes!"

"You wanted me inside of you?"

"Yes."

He pulls out, just his tip inside. I squeeze trying to pull him in more. "You are a greedy girl tonight..." He kisses my nose and stays just barely inside me. I start to squeeze my legs but he shakes his head, "No...You'll wait..."

"Please. Max...please..." I try my sweetest voice. *I want so badly to just pull him in again*!

He slams in, twice. I'm moaning louder until I realize he stopped again. "No! Please, please…" It's a full on whiny moan, I can't help myself. I actually manage to push against his arms even. He's smiling and pushing in just a little more from laughing.

Finally, he lets go of my wrists, puts his arm under my butt and pulls me hips up to him, forcing himself in me deeper. My moans are wilder, I come loudly as he fucks me fast and furious. I clutch at his shoulders again, pulling and pushing with him as much as I can. I'm coming again when he explodes, his own moan and grunts in my ear. He continues holding me to him, breathing heavily together.

When he finally moves his arm, my butt is throbbing...but so is my pussy. He stretches next to me on his side, head on his arm. I smile at his sweaty hair and run my finger through his waves. He puts his hand on my hip and squeezes my bone, smiling back.

I start to get up, but he stops me with more pressure on my hip. "No. Ask my permission before you leave my side." He's smiling, but I know he's serious. *This is a new rule.*

"Can I go to the bathroom?"

"Yes. You have five minutes."

I hurry to the bathroom. There's a jar of cream on the counter that wasn't there earlier. When I come back out, Max is sitting up in bed waiting for me. "What's this?" I show him the jar as I'm getting back into bed.

"My mom thought you might need it." He's grinning at me.

"Is it hand cream?" It's an unopened white jar that looks medicinally plain, no description or instructions, just 'Arnica' and a health food store label. I open it. It has a pleasant smell, but not much of one.

His smile gets bigger, a laugh in his voice, "It's for your bottom, baby."

I bolt my eyes up to his. I'm red all over. "You *told* her?!"

He laughs again slightly, "I didn't *have* to. It's *obvious* that you had a good spanking and your butt is still sore." He laughs as I turn even brighter red. "This is supposed to be soothing and helps with any bruising or redness. Would you like me to put some on you?" He's still laughing slightly.

"I don't think this is at all funny, Max!" I'm frowning, thinking that his mom is giving him creams... *I'm too embarrassed to even finish the thought in my own head.*

"No pouting, Lucy." His smile is gone. "Or I'll give you something to pout about." I stop frowning and only look embarrassed. "Now, roll over and I'll put some on you..." I do as he says; glad to have my face turned away, my hair hiding my redness.

Only the redness of my other cheeks is exposed now. I want to crawl under the covers and not show my face for the next two days.

He's gentle, rubbing so lightly, and the cream is cooling. His soothing touch lulls me into sleep. I wake long enough to mumble into my pillow, "Thank you," to his "Good night, sweet girl," and a kiss on my head.

I wake up early, the sun barely shining on the terrace. I never sleep on my stomach, but I didn't move all night. I feel a thousand times better this morning. My thighs only have a slight twinge of muscle stiffness and my butt feels almost normal, except for the deep red spot just above my thighs. *It will be days before that's back to normal.* I see the jar on the nightstand and take this into the bathroom to take a look at myself. *Yep...still very red.*

I rub gently with the cream. It does seem to help. *But I refuse to thank his mom. Max can punish me for being rude, but I cannot deal with that much embarrassment.*

Max didn't allow me to pack any shorts, just dresses. I choose a simple cotton one and leave my hair loose.

I head down the stairs, but don't hear anyone. *Max must be running.*

I know Max would be proud of me if I make coffee and get breakfast ready, so I head into the kitchen. A small light is on above the nearly full coffee pot. The aroma of fresh brew is heaven to my growling stomach. I beeline for it.

"I just made some."

I jump and yell, "Holy shit!" with my hand to my chest.

Jake is laughing at me from the terrace doors. "Better not let Max hear you talk like that."

"You...you scared me." My heart is only just calming, my hand still on my chest. His words make my heart race a little again though. I look around guiltily to see if Max is near.

"He's not here." He continues laughing a little at me, a strange smile on his face. "He was on his way out for a run when I got here."

"Oh..." I just turn to get a cup out of the cabinet.

"Do you mind...?" I turn and he's standing with his cup out, the same strange crooked smile on his face. He hasn't moved from the door.

"Oh...um...of course..." I walk the pot over to him and pour some in his half-full cup. I look up at him just as he takes a sip. He has the same height, same waves, same crooked grin as his brother. This close I can see that his eyes have the same flecks of gold too, and his smell is soapy-musk. *So like Max's.*

I step backwards before turning around with the pot. I take my time pouring myself some. "I didn't know you were coming up this weekend, Jake..."

"I decided last minute. Nobody knew. I know Dad has his final day of summer planned out, so I came early to avoid the traffic and be here for the fun." He lifts his coffee cup to me.

I stand with my back against the cabinet, holding my mug under my nose, a shield from him.

He continues smiling at me for a while, until I lower my eyes. "You look very pretty this morning, Lucy." I jolt at this. I'm not sure how I should respond. *It's another man giving me a compliment, but it's Max's brother, so...*

"Thank you," I say it quietly, shyly.

He just smiles the same and turns to the terrace again. "I love watching the sun come up over the lake."

"Me too." I follow him outside and stand next to him against the rail. The water is already fading from golden, the sun above it. But the sky is a collage of pinks and blues still. We stand silently sipping and watching for a while.

Finally, Jake turns and pulls out a chair. He waits for me to take the seat. I do, still unsure how to react to him. Jake sits next to me at the end of the cedar table.

"How've you been?" I ask first, so he doesn't.

He laughs. "Well...I've been shitty, thanks for asking." He rubs his jaw, stubble visible from here. "No...Really, I'm okay. It was rough at first. Getting my stuff out of the apartment was easy at least. Julia threw most of it into the hall in a drunken rage that night."

"I'm so sorry. That's awful."

"She has quite a temper." He shakes his head. "The breakup...it was a long time coming." He looks directly at me.

"Max has been trying to reach you. He wanted to help." I keep looking at my cup, keeping my hands on it, like I'm cold. Really, I just don't know what to do with them. I keep wanting to touch Jake's arm, to comfort him.

"I know. I talked to him a little before you came down. I just couldn't be around anyone. I needed to sort everything out for myself." He leans back in his chair, sipping his coffee, so relaxed.

"And did you...sort things out?" *I wish I could relax*. I feel tightly wound, waiting for him to say something to me about Max.

"Ha...that's gonna take a while I think." His laugh is rich and deep, like Max's. "But I have a sublease for the next five months and I have all my stuff. And I know that it was for the best." He stops to give me an appraising look. "She wasn't the right girl for me...too ambitious, too assertive. I tried, but...well, we tried. Julia will be happier too."

I only nod.

"How bout you? How are you and Max doing?" He's still staring at me.

"We're great." I don't want to talk anymore with Jake about Max. Our last talk was stressful enough.

"That's great." I shoot my eyes up at him, then quickly back to my cup. "Ya know...if you ever need to talk… I'll listen."

"I don't think Max would like that." I say this quietly though. His kindness always throws me off.

He leans in, "Would *you* like it?"

I shoot him another look. *Damn him and his kindness!* "I don't need to talk, Jake. I'm *fine*." He says nothing only looks at me with that same concerned niceness, so I feel I have to say more to stop any further discussions. "Max and I are fine."

"Good. I'm happy for you then. Both of you." And he actually sounds like he means it. He sits back and smiles at me. "I've been thinking a lot about you."

I gulp and blink at this, but say nothing.

"I've been thinking that…well, you may have the wrong impression of me."

"What impression is that?" I can finally speak, but I keep the cup up to my face, my shield again.

"That I'm so different from Max…" He nods at my startled look. "I never liked how driven Julia was. I always thought that…well, that she'd come around. That we'd get married and have a life together." He shakes his head, looking over mine for a moment before continuing. "I fooled myself into thinking that it would work out just because I wanted it to."

"I'm sorry…I…didn't know that she hadn't told you about the travel." I still feel guilty that I knew about the job and he didn't.

He smiles at me. "I don't blame you. I knew. I just fooled myself, like I said." He appraises me again. "But I won't make that mistake again." His look becomes more piercing, making me squirm a little. *So like Max.* "I have a better idea of what I want…going forward."

I tear my eyes away from his, just as Alex and Ron walk out to the terrace together. Jake stands up looking a little sheepish. "Oh my goodness!" Alex runs over to give Jake a hug and kiss. "This is a great surprise."

"Glad you could make it, Jake." Ron also hugs him. *The prodigal son returns triumphantly.*

I hear Max come in the front door. He comes out to the terrace and smiles at me, winking. "One big happy family again." Jake pushes his shoulder.

"I should get breakfast in the oven then." I jump up and circle around the four of them. Max grabs my arm and pulls me into a hug. "Eww...you're all sweaty!" But I'm smiling, snuggling into his wet shirt more. He lets go and I head inside.

"Need any help?" It's Jake asking.

"She's fine." Max answers. I don't turn around, just keep walking. I don't want to see either of their faces.

"This is great, Lucy." Jake is taking a third helping of my egg croissant casserole. Ron and Max both had seconds already. Ron said he loved it. Alex already thanked me and said it was very good. She said this like a judge at the county fair giving me a ribbon for a job well done. And I felt very proud of myself for it.

Max puts his hand on my knee; he's proud of me too. "You better get going on a shower." He already took one while I was cooking. I start to pout thinking that we won't be able to take one together, but I hide it behind a napkin before anyone can see.

"I should help with dishes." I start to get up with my dish, but see the look on Max's face. I realize that I just contradicted him and almost sit back down. Instead, I stand there frozen for a second until Ron rescues me.

"Jake...you haven't been around for chores much lately. You're on clean up!"

"Great... This is what I get for making the long drive to spend the day with my family." But he's also getting up with his finished dish. He takes my plate out of my hand and smiles knowingly at me. I feel a knot forming. I avoid looking at Max again and hurry back inside.

After I messed up at the table, I'm quiet. Max has been smiling at me and his hand has been on my knee for the whole drive, but I don't want to upset him at all.

I got ready in record time, trying to show in my speediness how sorry I was for not doing what he said right away. I put on his favorite dress and left my hair down too.

"Have I told you how pretty you are today, baby?"

"Only a few times." Despite my uneasiness at displeasing him earlier, Max's praise always makes me smile. He winks at me and I'm the happiest girl in the world.

I have no idea where we're going. He wouldn't tell me. I know we have to be back for a sunset cruise with Ron, the end of summer ride Jake told me about. It looks like we have the whole day to ourselves though, and I couldn't be happier. I'm still hungry for Max's attention.

We've followed the shoreline of the lake, getting snapshots of watery sunshine. The main road isn't busy, despite the holiday, but it's still slow going. Max turns off to a side street, heading away from the lake. Traffic thins even more and I relax. I close my eyes and ignore the bumps in the road. I'm almost used to the numbed pain of my butt. *My, what a spanking will do to a girl.* I fall into a deep sleep, slumping in the seat with my head leaning towards Max.

"Wake up, sleepy," Max is petting my head, smiling at me. It takes me a second to realize that I'm not in my dream, that we're not back in his apartment.

"Where are we?" I sit up stiffly, my neck crink fighting with my butt soreness for first dibs on my sympathy. I can see a blanket and basket set up in front of the car a ways.

"Wow...you were out cold." He laughs. "You only slept for a minute though." He gets out and comes over to my side. I let him lift me out of the car, keeping his arms around my back and kissing me. "We're at our perfect picnic spot."

The sun is bright and I blink away the drowsy remnants of my dreams. We walk hand-in-hand over to the blanket. "You did all this?" The basket is open and I can see a full lunch inside with chicken, sides, bread, and lemonade. "Thank you." I squeeze him next to me.

I start to sit down. "Wait." I stop. He runs back to the car and grabs the pillow from my side. He hands me the pillow with his brow raised, a grin, "You've been punished enough." I thank him again, smiling.

I have no idea where we are, but there's no one around. We're covered by trees, but have an amazing view of the lake. I can't even hear any traffic sounds. We're next to each other, close on the blanket, me on my pillow, him on his side, stretched out.

I reach into the basket and start pulling everything out. The fried chicken smells great, leftovers from dinner yesterday. There's even a piece of apple pie to share. My mouth is watering already. I get the napkins, plates and silverware off the bottom. "This is the most perfect picnic I've ever seen. And the most perfect spot. Thank you again," I lean over and kiss him.

He pulls me into a deeper kiss, his hand behind my neck. "I want to make everything perfect for you, Lucy." His eyes are intense, his voice soft. I forget about the lunch and slide down to be stretched next to him, looking up into his eyes. He moves closer, pressing against my side, his right arm moving under my neck to prop my head up. His left hand goes to my hip, pressing on my bone. I breathe in his scent as he leans in for a kiss. I hold my breath while his tongue explores what he knows so well. He lifts his head slightly and smiles at me. "You are perfect for me, Lucy. And you're all mine."

"I am all yours, Max." I put my arms around his neck and pull him down for another kiss.

25 Him

I can feel her hunger; her need for my attention. *She's as needy as she was yesterday.* Her body presses into me, her hands pulling my hair. I know what she wants. *But she'll have to wait.* I pull my face back. "We better eat..." Her look of disappointment almost makes me laugh. I kiss her nose. "Be a good girl and finish getting lunch ready."

She immediately sits up, repositions the pillow and starts putting everything on plates for us. When she has everything ready, she smiles at me. "How's this?"

"Almost perfect." She frowns and I have to rub her cheek. *So expressive, my Lucy.* I move to sit in front of her, knees bent, sitting back on my heels. "Here." I hand her one of the napkin-wrapped silverware sets. She relaxes and smiles.

I watch her unroll the napkin in her lap slowly. Still on the middle of the fork handle, the ring sparkles in the sunshine. She looks up surprised, slowly smiling.

"What...what's this, Max?" She leaves the set open on her lap, only looking at me.

Grinning, I pick up the silverware and drop the ring into my hand, leaving the rest by my side; my eyes are on hers the whole time. I take her hand and hold the ring ready to put on her, "I want you to be my wife, Lucy." I smile. "Say yes."

"Yes!" She shakes, tears already forming, her right hand going to her mouth, while she watches as I put the ring on her finger.

I put my hands on the sides of her face and pull her up to me, both of us on our knees facing each other, kissing. Her arms circle my waist and she clings to me. "You've made me so happy, Max!"

"I'll make you happy for the rest of our lives, baby." I kiss her head.

She suddenly pulls away and puts her left hand out. "It's so beautiful." The diamond is bigger than her knuckle, shining brightly in the sun. It's a single solitary beauty, like my Lucy, an emerald cut diamond sitting across her finger; it's a large stamp of my possessiveness. "Thank you." Her eyes are wet as she looks from me to the ring.

"I want to give you the world, baby." I sit back with my legs stretched out. I pull her onto my lap, her legs stretching behind me, and kiss her again. She rubs against my cock, already hard. I know we're in a deserted area, no one around for miles.

Pushing her back slightly, I pull her thong down to her upper thighs and I undo my shorts. Her hands grab my hair, pulling. I smile and pick her up, positioning her over my cock and slowly lowering her onto me. She moans a deep cry.

With my arm supporting her back, picking her up again and pushing us both onto the blanket, I'm on top of her, her legs wrapped firmly around my legs. She meets my thrusts with her hips, squeezing just the way I like each time. It doesn't take long before we're fucking full speed, full force, both heads back, yelling as we finish.

I hold her head against mine. "I love you."

"I love you.... fiancé!" She smiles and her laugh pushes me out of her.

I sit up and back. Lucy stays laying down stretching her left arm straight up, moving it in the sun, staring at the ring on her finger. "You like it?" I smile watching her. *My soon-to-be-wife.*

She sits up, her eyes jumping to mine. "Oh, yes, very much, Max...I love that I'm going to be your wife and get to wear this for the rest of my life." She smiles wickedly for a second, "I love that I get to be Mrs. Lucy Shannon-Traeger." She laughs at my frown and puts her left hand on my cheek. "I'm just kidding."

"Not funny." I grab her and pull her onto my lap. She keeps smiling at her left hand on my chest. "You will be Mrs. Max Traeger."

"I like the sound of that..." She hasn't stopped playing with her ring in the sun.

I smile looking down on her. *She'll make a good wife...with a few more lessons.*

She tilts her head up to me, smiling too. "What are you thinking?"

"I'm thinking what a wonderful wife you'll make me." Her head stays tilted, her smile bigger. "My dutiful, submissive, and obedient Mrs. Traeger."

Max and Lucy continue their story in

True Choices.

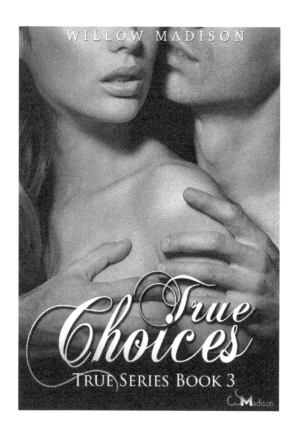

1 Her

The drive back to the house seems shorter. *Maybe because I'm distracted by the rock on my finger.* I giggle to myself, stealing a look at Max, who has his hand in my lap. I put my left hand over his, the ring still shines in the lowering sunshine.

I can't believe all that has happened in such a short time. My head is literally swimming. Oh, my God, I need to stop screaming in my head. I laugh and Max turns his head to smile at me, squeezing my thigh.

We went from the bottom of my betrayal two days ago, to the depths of his anger, to this. We're engaged. *And I'm the luckiest girl in the world. I get to be Mrs. Max Traeger.*

I squeeze his hand and Max smiles again, keeping his eyes on the thick holiday traffic. I know he doesn't want to keep his family waiting. We have plans for an afternoon ride around the lake. Max is very punctual. Being late is a serious pet-peeve.

I've learned about all of his pet-peeves. *Well, rules really.* I swallow. Looking at my beautiful ring, taking up most of my finger, like a large brick, I know that I might as well be honest with myself. I have rules to follow. Being his wife, I will probably have even more rules to follow. And more consequences if I don't.

I shift in my seat. Even with the small pillow Max allowed me, the lowest part of my butt still hurts from when he spanked me two days ago. I shudder just thinking about how angry I made him. I don't ever want to get him that angry again. It took him all night to finally forgive me.

"Lucy, are you cold?" Max saw me shudder and is raising the car windows.

"No. I'm fine." I smile at his attentiveness. He always notices everything. "Thank you."

I'd broken so many of his rules on Saturday, I'm still ashamed. And I tested him, to see if he'd let me get away with acting like I could do as I please around my friends. *I won't make that mistake again*!

I left my phone at his parent's lake house. I didn't want to see all the missed calls and messages from Tracy and Laura. I've been ignoring them since Saturday. I know what they want to say anyway.

I'd misbehaved, *monumentally*, at our company picnic. And they saw Max's angry reaction. They heard me apologize to him and call him Sir. Tracy flipped out. I almost laugh remembering how red her face was; it matched her hair. And Laura...I think she was just more shocked than anything.

I don't want to think about them now, though. Not today. I pull my left hand up again and watch the ring sparkle.

Max laughs at me. "You're going to go blind staring at that."

"You don't think...it's too big?" The ring is very simple. It's a simple platinum band with one simply large diamond that sits horizontally across my finger. Max was very proud to tell me all about picking out the stone and setting himself. He had this made just for me. The engraving says, "Always," just like the watch he gave me.

Max takes my left hand and kisses my palm. This never fails to send little shockwaves down my stomach. He's so tender and gentle. "No. I told my jeweler that I wanted everyone in a fifty-block radius to know you're mine. I think it'll do the job." He winks at me.

We pull into the gravel drive of the house. I'm suddenly very nervous.

We've had the day to ourselves, the most perfect day. I've been able to daydream about our wedding and our life together. But this is reality. We have to tell his parents, his brother. I don't know how they'll react. We've only known each other for such a short time. *Oh, God. I'm going to have to tell my parents and brother.*

I'm starting to feel a little queasy as I watch Max come around to open my door. His smile falters when I'm standing next to him and he sees that I'm not smiling anymore.

He pushes his body into mine against the closed car door. With both hands on the sides of my face, he kisses me and whispers into my ear, "You'll be fine."

He always knows what I'm thinking. He says he loves that I'm so expressive. "What if...what if they don't really want you to marry me?" I know the opinion of his family, especially his dad's, is very important to him.

"Relax," he takes my hand and we walk towards the steps. I try to breathe a little deeper, but feel like I'm choking on my dry throat.

Inside, we can hear laughter coming from the terrace. I follow slowly behind Max through the house and stop at the French doors. I try to stay hidden behind him, but Max won't let me. He steps aside and puts his arm around my shoulder, pushing me forward with him. All three Traegers are staring at us; I look at my feet instead of meeting anyone's eyes.

"Well?" Ron, his dad, speaks first.

"Say hello to your future daughter-in-law." I swallow and jump my eyes up to Max. He's beaming with such happiness and pride that for a second I don't even hear anything else.

Alex, his mom, jumps up from her seat and runs around to us, grabbing me and hugging me to her chest. "Congratulations! We're so excited!" She grabs my hand and says how beautiful the ring is.

Ron stands and shakes Max's hand congratulating him, before turning to me and putting his arms out. I hesitate before squeezing back his embrace. This is the closest I've been to the man. He's only shook my hand before, very formal. It's where Max gets all of his rules and old fashioned ways, from Ron.

He's nearly as tall as Max and I can feel that his back and stomach muscles are strong. He doesn't let go, holding me in a side hug, while Alex continues hugging and kissing Max. "Jake, get up and congratulate your brother and his bride." I jump at the edge in Ron's voice. So like Max's.

I've avoided looking at his brother. He always puts me on edge. This morning wasn't any different. His mix of kindness and something else...like he's looking through me. I hear the chair scrape the deck, but keep my eyes down.

"Congratulations, Max. I'm sure you'll both be very happy." He hugs Max and I steal a look. They are brothers in a mirror, same dark waves, green eyes, tall and muscled. Max's hair is shorter, his eyes lighter, but they could be twins. Only three years apart, Max is older at 35. He loves to mock Jake by calling him "little brother." I drop my eyes again before Jake turns to me.

Ron lets go and I sway a little. I've locked my knees to stop from shaking and held my breath for too long. Jake grabs me in a hug, but doesn't press against me, just holds me up with his strong arms. He kisses my head, tenderly, "You'll make a beautiful bride, Lucy." He lets go when Max stands next to me again.

I finally look at Jake when he sits back down, watching us. His look is almost unreadable, but I can see a hint of something, a little darkness. I turn away and bury my face in Max's chest. I'm sure Jake is thinking about Julia. Our happiness has to hurt in the face of his recent break-up with her.

"So, have you decided any details...?" Ron is sitting back down. Alex has run off towards the kitchen.

I'm surprised when Max answers, "We'll get married next month." He smiles at the stunned look on my face. I glance at Jake but look away just as quick when I see his matching shocked look. "I haven't decided where. One of the LPE places in the city maybe." Max's voice sounds far away to me. I can't grasp that he's discussing our wedding so matter-of-factly. *We haven't discussed any of this*.

Alex is returning with a tray of glasses and an iced bucket of champagne. I remember seeing this on the counter when we walked in. It only just dawns on me that they knew all along that Max was going to propose today. And they knew I'd say yes. "What about having it here...on the lawn?" She sets the tray in front of Ron.

"That's a great idea," Ron is opening the champagne, the pop is soft but I still jump. I feel like I'm watching from a distance. "We could get a tent...do something to make it real nice."

"I'll think about it. I can get one or more of the LPE restaurants to cater, but this might be a little too much of a drive. Could be nice as long as the weather holds up, though." Max holds a chair for me to sit and I'm glad to take it. My knees feel a little shaky still. He keeps talking about which of the restaurants he would most likely use. Since he's a partner in the largest restaurant/bar owner/management group in the city, he can have his choice.

"What do *you* want, Lucy?" Jake is sitting on the other side of the table from me. The dark blue water of Lake

Michigan frames his shoulders and face. He spoke very quietly, but all eyes turn to him, then me.

"I..." I swallow and say in small voice, "I don't know...I...we haven't talked about all that yet..." I shoot my eyes at Max. He hands me a glass of champagne with a wink.

"To my Lucy. To our future." Everyone raises a glass; Jake last. I take a big sip.

Jake downs his and reaches for more. "Take it easy, son. You're driving the boat tonight." Ron says this with that same edge to his deep voice. *Max is so like him.*

I think Jake's going to say something back for a second. Instead, he stops pouring and mumbles, "Yes, Sir."

"And you two better change...it'll probably be a little chillier on the water." Alex is nodding at Max and me.

Max stands up and pulls my chair for me. I take another big gulp before setting my glass down and getting up.

Going up the stairs, I watch how the light catches the ring. It definitely gets attention, just like Max wanted. *No mistaking that I'm taken.* This makes me smile and relax again.

At least his family seemed happy; that went better than I expected. At the top of the stairs, I turn and put my arms around his neck. He's still a little taller than me, but I can easily kiss his forehead. He picks me up around my waist and carries me backwards towards our room, kissing.

"Get changed quickly." He swats my butt, eliciting a small yelp, since it's still sore. "You still have to call your family."

Oh, God. Why did he have to remind me?! "I can do that when we get back..."

His smile changes slightly, a little more crooked, a little frown to his brow. I hurry over to my suitcase and pull out the long dress I brought. Max wouldn't let me bring any pants or shorts. He likes me to look girlie and feminine. I'd rather be wearing jeans and a sweatshirt on the water, but I don't have any choice.

It's the end of summer; the nights are already crisping. The three-quarter sleeve, long cotton dress is the best option I brought. I have a long wool cardigan too. "How's this?" I turn so Max can see me. He's just pulling on a V-neck sweater over his head, the deep olive color compliments his eyes.

He grins, "You look great...but you're still going to freeze. I'll get a scarf and gloves for you from Mom." He starts to leave, but turns at the door and nods with a stern look again towards the dresser, "Your phone's over there."

I walk slowly over to it. I have five missed calls; I don't look to see the details. Ten new text messages that I ignore as well. I pick my parents out of the long list of contacts.

Dad picks up. "Hi, Dad. It's Lucy." I try to put all the happiness I was feeling earlier into my voice again.

"Hey, sweetheart." He pulls his mouth away from the phone a little, "Lizzie! It's Lucy on the phone." Dad hurts my ear yelling into the background for Mom.

Mom picks up another phone loudly. "Hi, sweetie! ...How's your visit going?" She sounds abnormally excited to hear from me.

I take a deep breath and hold it for a second. "I have some news..." My voice sounds extra high to me.

Mom actually squeals in high-pitched excitement, but Dad says calmly, "Let her *tell* us first, Lizzie..."

"Max and I are engaged." I say it slowly, waiting to hear their reaction. They've only met him once.

Mom squeals again and Dad says, "Okay, *now* you can congratulate her."

Mom starts gushing, "Oh that's such great news, Lucy. Congratulations. Max is such a wonderful man*!" I was not expecting this much excitement from her. I know she wants me to be married with a passel of grandkiddies on the way, but...*

"You knew?"

"Max called me yesterday. He's a very formal young man. He asked me for your hand." Dad sounds proud. *Of course Max would ask my dad's permission first. He is very traditional.*

Mom is still giggling on her phone. "He actually used those words, too," she giggles more, "Max didn't say when he was going to ask, but I was hoping we wouldn't have to sit on this news for long! Oh, honey, I'm so happy for you."

"Thanks, Mom."

"Congratulations, sweetheart." Dad sounds like he's tearing up.

"So...details. How did he ask?" Mom's excitement is still running high.

I want to tell her that he didn't ask, technically. He *told* me to say yes. "It was very romantic. He took me to a secluded hilltop above the lake. We had the most perfect picnic and he had the ring wrapped inside a napkin with the silverware. I was completely surprised."

"That is so sweet." Mom still has giggle-fever. Dad only coughs his approval, trying to act like he's not wiping his eyes and nose on his end. His little girl is getting married, after all. "What's the ring look like?"

Huge! "Very pretty, simple...a big solitaire. I'll take a picture with my phone and email it to you."

"Can't wait to see it!" She's obviously moved to be in the same room as Dad; there's an echo now. "Have you two talked about when you want to have the wedding?"

Max has. "We haven't had a chance. Um...but I don't think it's going to be a long engagement, Mom." *Max doesn't like to wait for anything.* "I'll let you know as soon as we decide anything, okay?"

"That sounds fine, sweetheart," Dad answered, "Just give us enough time to work out paying for everything. I have that fund your mom started when you were just a baby...we'll have to see what we need to do to close that out, Lizzie." They're talking to each other more than me now.

"Dad? Mom?" They're still talking to each other. "I have to go...Max is waiting for me. ...Mom?"

"Oh. Okay, sweetie. Call us as soon as you can." She kisses into the phone, an echo that pierces my ear. "And send that picture!" She hangs up.

"Congratulations again, sweetheart. Give our best to Max too." Dad hangs up after I say I will.

I put the phone down and hold my forehead. I'm feeling a little fuzzy from all the excitement. This whole holiday weekend has been a rollercoaster of emotions.

"Why didn't you tell them we're getting married next month?" I jump hearing Max's voice from the door.

"I...we...we haven't really talked about anything yet." I'm holding my hand to my chest. I can see the ring sparkling up at me.

"We're getting married next month, Lucy." His face is stern, set.

"I don't think my dad can...I don't think they can afford that, Max." I hear the whine and plea in my voice.

He frowns quizzically at me, like I just said something odd. "*I'm* paying for everything, of course. Your parents don't have to worry about *any* of that. They just need to be here to be a part of our wedding."

"But I don't...I mean...I can't plan a wedding in only a month. I don't even know what all to do." I'm laughing a little. I can't believe I'm pushing for a later date. But the thought of a big wedding in only four short weeks is overwhelming.

"We're getting married next month and that's final." He turns and walks away. I wait before following him downstairs.

I know Max likes being in control, but...but this is our wedding. This is the rest of our lives together. Maybe I'll try to talk to him again when we're back in the city. We really need to make *some* decisions together.

But I know I'm kidding myself. Max doesn't just *like* being in control. Max *is* in control. Period. *That's* final.